Definitely Not Sexy

Definitely
Not Sexy

* * * * * * * * *

JANE SUTTON

LITTLE, BROWN AND COMPANY
Boston   Toronto   London

Also by Jane Sutton
Confessions of an Orange Octopus
Me and the Weirdos
Not Even Mrs. Mazursky
What Should a Hippo Wear?

Copyright © 1988 by Jane Sutton

ALL RIGHTS RESERVED. NO PART OF THIS BOOK MAY BE RE-
PRODUCED IN ANY FORM OR BY ANY ELECTRONIC OR ME-
CHANICAL MEANS, INCLUDING INFORMATION STORAGE AND
RETRIEVAL SYSTEMS, WITHOUT PERMISSION IN WRITING
FROM THE PUBLISHER, EXCEPT BY A REVIEWER WHO MAY
QUOTE BRIEF PASSAGES IN A REVIEW.

FIRST EDITION

Library of Congress Cataloging-in-Publication Data

Sutton, Jane.
    Definitely not sexy / by Jane Sutton. — 1st ed.
        p.   cm.
Summary: After her induction into the Junior Honor Society,
Diana tries to change her image to fit into the Dumb Sexies
group at high school.
    ISBN 0-316-82325-2
    [1. Identity — Fiction.   2. High schools — Fiction.
3. Schools — Fiction.]   I. Title.
    PZ7.S96824De   1988
    [Fic] — dc19   88-18127
                                                        CIP
                                                        AC
10 9 8 7 6 5 4 3 2 1

FG

The characters and events portrayed in this book are ficti-
tious. Any similarity to real persons, living or dead, is coinci-
dental and not intended by the author.

Published simultaneously in Canada
by Little, Brown & Company (Canada) Limited
PRINTED IN THE UNITED STATES OF AMERICA

To Mr. Dannay, an extraordinary teacher who inspired me to question everything

Definitely Not Sexy

1

If there's one thing I've learned in my first semester of ninth grade, it's that there's no such thing as being smart and sexy. You're either one or the other. At least, that's the way it is at Beechurst High School.

I would love to be sexy. But what am I instead? Smart.

And now, thanks to yesterday's homeroom announcements, the whole school knows that Diana Pushkin (me) is smart, boring, goody-goody, unsexy . . . don't get me started.

Yesterday began something like this:

I sat down in homeroom, as usual, about three seconds before the late bell went off.

"Good morning, Diana," said Paula Proomer, who sits in front of me every day because Mr. ("Ass")

Aston makes us sit in alphabetical order (Paulo to Rooterman).

"Here we are, back at the dump," I mumbled.

Paula came out with one of her husky laughs, giving the entire male population of homeroom 9-7 an excuse to look at her. She was wearing one of those tight sweaters of hers that call attention to her nipples poking up underneath. Paula has more sweaters than anyone I've ever known. And her breasts may not be the largest in the ninth grade, but they're definitely the pointiest.

Paula is also blessed with huge bright-green movie-star eyes, which look even bigger and greener because of the generous amount of eye makeup she wears. Her hair is jet-black and wavy and cascades halfway down her back. She is at least five-foot-six.

And there I sit or, rather, *slump* behind her — four-eleven, a little overweight, bowlegged, with super straight light-brown hair that's cut short like a little cap on my head and, on my chin, a couple of pimples (the kind that are too bumpy to hide under cover-up), just to make me feel even better about myself.

Paula looks about eighteen, and I could pass for ten. Well, let's say ten and a half. Maybe my pimples make me look a little older.

At exactly 8:14, the morning announcements came crackling over the P.A. There was the usual garbage about macaroni and cheese and buttered green beans for lunch.

"Mmm!" I said. The kids around me laughed.

"Keep it down, *stew*dents!" said Mr. ("Ass") Aston, who was probably afraid someone would miss the vital news that the Chess Club meeting had been changed to Tuesday, December eleventh, and that there would be tryouts for Girls' Intramural Volleyball next Wednesday, December twelfth.

The kids in the Chess Club and Girls' Intramural Volleyball are not exactly part of the in-crowd, or the Sexies, as my friend Heidi Kellermeier and I call them. Who's sexy and who isn't is our favorite topic of conversation. Of the girls, Paula Proomer, as you may have guessed, is Definitely Sexy. So are Sarah Kates and Maggie Wallace. Sally Marverstein, Cynthia Rosen, and Roseanne Capullo are Moderately Sexy. Our friend Wendy Moroney, who has silky blond hair, a tall, slim body, and a carefree personality, is Slightly Sexy.

Our own names don't come up much in these discussions. That's because Heidi and I are good friends. And neither of us would want to depress the other by talking about what category *we* fit into, which is *Definitely* Not Sexy.

Maybe something good would rub off on us if we had a chance to hang out with the Sexies once in a while. But there's this thing called tracking in

Beechurst High School. All the kids like Heidi and me who got good grades in junior high and who scored well on these boring, asinine tests where you could sprain your wrist filling in tiny boxes with a pencil are in "honors" classes together. And everybody else is in regular classes — which means that, except during lunch, gym, health, and homeroom, I'm stuck with smart, well-behaved, Definitely Not Sexy kids like myself. I only get to see Wendy during lunch and gym. She's too busy getting high to do well in school.

After the fascinating announcement about Intramural Volleyball (you wouldn't catch *me* at those tryouts: my idea of an athletic experience is winding my watch) came a reminder to buy goodies at a bake sale to benefit the foreign-exchange program.

"Hey, week-old cupcakes again!" I had fun commenting to Cynthia Rosen, next to me. But when I heard the next announcement, I wasn't in such a yukking-it-up mood.

"Congratulations to the following students, who have been selected for induction into the Junior Honor Society next Friday. Please attend the preliminary rehearsal this afternoon. . . ."

I felt deathly ill. There was no way I wouldn't be one of the inductees. To be in this big-deal organization, you need an A− average and favorable recommendations from all your teachers. I hadn't gotten anything *less* than A— in the first two marking periods of high school. It wasn't that I'd studied hard; good grades just seem to come naturally to me.

I prayed that one of my teachers had given me an unsatisfactory recommendation. Hadn't I made one too many wisecracks in health class, for instance?

There were eleven names announced: David Cotter, Barbara Flynn, Terry Freid, Heidi Kellermeier, Richie Kessler, Steven Lawson, Sue Melvin, Billy Munson, Lisa Norris, Tammy Oliver, and (ugh) Diana Pushkin.

Let's face it, I'm up Creep creek.

"Congratulations, Diana!" Paula Proomer turned around to say.

"Thanks," I said, trying not to cry.

"I never knew you were such a brain," Danny Rickovsky said to me. He might as well have been saying, "Gee, I didn't know you had lice."

Terrific, I thought. Heidi and I had decided that Danny Rickovsky, with his gorgeous dimples and his yellow-brown eyes, was the sexiest boy in the ninth grade. Now I'd have absolutely no chance with him, or with anyone else, for that matter. Now I'd be hopelessly branded as smart and Definitely Not Sexy.

"Well, *stew*dents, it seems we have a celebrity in our homeroom," said Mr. ("Ass") Aston with one of his tilted smiles. He looked at me and started to clap, and so, to my profound embarrassment, did everyone else. I couldn't tell whether they were genuinely congratulating me or making fun of me for being a Creep. Probably the latter.

All the commotion stirred Doug Randow (toward the front of the next row, between Quincy and Rifkin) from his usual drug-induced oblivion. "What's the noise?" he asked, sounding as if he were calling Beechurst long-distance from outer space.

"Diana Pushkin made the Junior Honor Society!" explained Kathy Preston, who is Moderately Sexy.

Doug echoed my sentiments exactly. "Big deal," he said.

"It *is* a big deal!" piped up Kathy, who is dumb enough to think it is.

"Yeah, Doug!" said Cynthia Rosen, who is another Sexy. "Good work, Diana!"

I was too mortified to answer. Cynthia had probably been thinking, Poor little Creep — I'll say something nice and brighten her day.

When the bell rang, four guys, including Danny Rickovsky, gathered around Paula Proomer. I could see them looking her up and down. And I just knew they all wanted to fool around with her. I started imagining the wild parties she must have when her parents are out. Come to think of it, someone like her probably doesn't have parents. How could you face your mom and dad if you looked like that? It would be too embarrassing.

8

I imagined Paula melting against Danny Rickovsky in a long, hot embrace. It would be just like The Movies.

I can't wait to start fooling around with boys. But I don't know when I'll ever get the opportunity, especially now that I've been condemned to the Junior Honor Society. My biggest sexual encounter so far was at a puny sixth-grade kissing party, which doesn't really count at all. I've never even Frenchkissed or had my breasts touched (except by accident in the hall).

My friend Wendy actually went all the way with a counselor in camp last summer. She told me all about it. But she's done lots of things I don't have the nerve to do.

Heidi says *she's* in no hurry to get "sexually involved" with anyone. She plans to wait until she falls in love, and then it will be "so much more beautiful." I keep telling her I don't want to wait that long.

As I slunk into the crowded hall after homeroom, I saw Danny Rickovsky put his arm around Paula. How I wished he would leave her to one of her other admirers, strut over to me, and say, "Hey, Diana, you think you're so smart? How about coming with me to one of Paula's parties, and I'll teach *you* a thing or two?" I would leap at the chance. Yes, I would.

2

At the after-school rehearsal, I found out that the Junior Honor Society assembly would be even worse than I'd imagined. First of all, we have to wear horrible, loose-fitting black gowns that go over our clothes. We look like huge cowbells. And we have to hold candles to "symbolize the Light of Knowledge."

Mr. Altamatto, who's the faculty adviser to the Junior Honor Society, was all excited about the Light of Knowledge routine. I thought it was the corniest thing I'd ever heard.

"Be sure to stand tall!" he told us about six times.

Well, it's hard to stand tall when you're four-eleven. And I'd rather sink into the ground than be seen on stage in front of the *442* ninth- and tenth-graders who are lucky enough *not* to be inducted into the Junior Honor Society. I HATE anything that calls attention to my being smart. And being displayed as a smart cowbell in front of 442 normal people is my idea of torture.

Big groups make me nervous anyway, though I wouldn't think they were so bad if I could make jokes or something. The Junior Honor Society assembly certainly doesn't sound like an occasion to crack jokes. It sounds so serious you could puke.

I was glad my friend Heidi was going through this misery with me.

"Can you believe this?" I whispered to her as Mr. Altamatto handed out the Candles of Knowledge at the rehearsal. Heidi has curly red hair and freckles. She's about four inches taller than I am, which means she's average height. She's kind of nice-looking, except her chin is too big, or too pushed out or something. I haven't been able to figure out what the problem is exactly, but her chin doesn't go with the rest of her face.

"I think the assembly is neat!" said Heidi. "I've been working hard all year, and it's nice to get recognition for a change."

"Recognition!" I shouted in a whisper. "For being the most boring people in the school, you mean. We'll never have a chance to be considered the tiniest bit sexy."

"You know, if I could choose between being smart and sexy, I'd still choose smart," said Heidi.

"No!" I said.

"Yes!" said Heidi with a self-important, freckled-nosed sniff.

The fact that my good friend, with whom I'd spent countless hours discussing the relative sexiness of various members of the Beechurst High School freshman class, was now content to be a hopeless Creep did nothing to improve my dark mood. I started to wonder why I'd gotten myself into such a boring niche. I mean, I know I'm sexy *inside*. But I go around in dull, babyish clothes and a mousy haircut. Why don't *I* wear green eye shadow and tight sweaters? What's to stop *me* from wearing tight-ass jeans and high heels?

Nothing. But *something* must be stopping me, because I can't imagine myself looking any other way.

By dinnertime, I felt a little better. My parents, Wilma and Zeke, are always interested in hearing what I've been doing and all. Even though I don't always *tell* them what I've been doing, it's nice to know they care. I'm the only kid in the family, and they think I'm pretty great just the way I am.

That night I wasn't in the most talkative mood,

since I didn't feel like bringing up the Junior Honor Society. I did enjoy Wilma's lasagna, though. Wilma is quite the cook.

"Have some more!" she said to me, more than once. And I did, more than once. It's no wonder I'm not exactly skinny.

Wilma and Zeke both had three helpings. Compared to them, I'm emaciated. To say that my parents are fat and have no waists is putting it kindly. To add that Zeke's belly looks as if he swallowed a whole watermelon and it got stuck there, and Wilma's looks as if she ate a soccer ball on a bet, is only a slight exaggeration. They both have dry brown hair, and Zeke wears clear-framed eyeglasses.

If there were a category for Hopelessly Not Sexy, that would be Wilma and Zeke's.

Just as I was about to bite into one of Wilma's fabulous brownies for dessert, the phone rang. I answered it, hoping it would be Wendy or Heidi wanting to get together over the weekend. Instead, it was a heavy-breather type. After a few noisy breaths to give me the idea, a low voice asked, "Want to shake your thing for me?"

I hung up.

"Who was that, Baby?" asked Wilma. Can you believe it? She still calls me Baby!

"It was an obscene call," her Baby blurted out. And then I thought, Why didn't I say that no one was there or it was a wrong number or it was some little kid making a phony phone call? I mean, my parents *never* talk about sex. I think the reason I'm an only child is that they had sex only once.

"What did he say?" asked Wilma, sounding like a little kid whose big sister had just showed her a book of dirty jokes.

"Nothing much," I said, looking at Zeke's suddenly bright-red forehead. I could feel my own face turn the same color.

"You know what I would have done?" said Wilma thoughtfully. "I would have repeated back to the caller exactly what he had said to me."

"I don't think so, Mom," I said. And I burst out laughing at the thought of Wilma firing back, "Want to shake your thing for me?" Zeke would probably choke on his brownie.

I wanted to change the subject, so I asked Wilma how little Ryan Kritchlow was doing. Ryan is a kid in the nursery school class Wilma teaches.

Wilma's eyes lit up. "He said the funniest thing today," she said. "Although I tried not to smile at the time. I caught him eating fun dough, and I told him fun dough is for playing with, not for eating. And you know what he said?" Wilma started to chuckle.

"What?" I asked.

"He said, 'Have you ever tasted it, Mrs. Pushkin?'

14

And I explained, 'No, because fun dough is not for eating, even though it looks nice and smells nice.' And that little imp said to me, 'Well, you really should try it, Mrs. Pushkin. You might like it. How do you know something is no good if you don't try it?' "

I laughed, partly because the story was funny and partly because I was relieved not to be discussing the Obscene Phone Call.

"That's cute," I said. "His parents must have given him that line about trying lima beans or something."

I looked over at Zeke to see if he was laughing too. Although he was methodically consuming brownies, his mind seemed to be several miles away. He was probably thinking about more creative ways to sell life insurance, which is what he does for a living. Zeke doesn't always notice what's going on in front of his rather long nose. For instance, the fact that I call him Zeke instead of Daddy goes right by him.

Wilma, however, doesn't miss a trick. And she has definitely noticed that I call her Wilma. She thinks it's fresh, disrespectful, inappropriate, and several other of her favorite adjectives.

"Oh, Wilma," I tell her, making her even angrier. "Don't you know it's the kids who call their mothers Mother or Mom who secretly hate their guts and do all kinds of stuff behind their backs?"

15

Wilma is not convinced by my argument, which happens to be true. For example, Wendy, who is by far my wildest friend, calls her mom Mother Dear. I, on the other hand, do hardly anything that I need to hide from Wilma and Zeke.

I don't know why I started calling them by their first names. Mainly because I wanted to be cool, I guess. Also because Wilma and Zeke are kind of funny names, and my parents are pretty cute in spite of their long list of faults. They're really quite lovable and kind. It makes me smile inside to say their names. Wilma and Zeke. Zeke and Wilma. Zilma and Weke.

"What are your plans for the weekend?" Wilma asked me as she cleared the dishes.

"Nothing much," I said. I had already finished my homework in study hall. (At least there are *some* advantages to being a "brain.") The fact that, as usual, I had no exciting weekend plans was not by choice. If I had the chance, I would be doing all kinds of outrageous things that would knock my parents' socks off. (Actually, Zeke probably wouldn't notice.)

"Well, you're welcome to come with us to garage sales tomorrow morning!" said Wilma.

"I think I'll pass," I said, glad to hear that my parents would be out the next morning. At least I'd have a chance to blast the living-room stereo and sing along with my new *Julie Paris in Concert* record.

The mention of garage sales miraculously brought Zeke back into the here and now. "Any good ones listed in the *Beechurst News?*" he asked. Behind his clear-framed eyeglasses, his eyes glistened with excitement. So did Wilma's. It was practically romantic.

You see, Wilma and Zeke get all their satisfaction from garage sales. They don't need a sex life. On Saturday mornings they get up bright and early to hit every sale in Beechurst and buy useless junk that it gives them mysterious pleasure to have spotted first. For example, Wilma has acquired the world's largest collection of trivets, which seem to take up every square inch of the kitchen walls. Half of them are chipped or faded, and almost all of them are ugly.

Wilma and I were on kitchen cleanup duty that night. Just as Zeke took off to watch a basketball game on TV, the phone rang.

"Hello?" I answered in a tentative voice, in case it was the heavy breather again.

Thank goodness, it was only Wendy this time. "Got anything going on two weeks from Saturday night?" she asked. "My brother and I are throwing a party when Mother and Father Dear take off for a weekend in the Poconos."

Wendy's parents are always going away for weekends and leaving her home with her big brother, Fred.

"Does a dog have fleas?" I said to Wendy. "Of course I'm free on a Saturday night." Then I whispered, so Wilma wouldn't hear, "Unless I die of embarrassment at the you-know-what assembly first."

"Come on, Diana, it won't be so bad," said Wendy. "A lot of kids look up to you for being such a hot student, you know. Including me."

"You look up to me? How could you possibly? I'm only four-eleven."

Wendy laughed. "Well, hey, *Heidi* is all excited about being in the Junior Honor Society. I was just talking to her. She even got an appointment with Jean-Pierre the day before the assembly."

Jean-Pierre is this hairdresser from France who Heidi thinks is a sensitive-looking genius. According to Heidi, he's a total authority on beauty. He's cut the hair of Broadway actresses and First Ladies. I don't know *what* he's doing in little old Beechurst.

"I'd rather have my hair *lengthened* than cut before the assembly," I told Wendy. "I'd like to grow it right over my face."

"Diana!" called Wilma, above the sound of water running in the kitchen sink. "We're supposed to be a cleanup *team*!"

"I have to go, Wen," I said. "I'll look forward to

your party." I wasn't just saying that. Wendy was sure to invite some sexy types I didn't usually hang out with. Maybe I'd have a chance to do some things my parents wouldn't approve of.

"So," said Wilma, as I dried and she washed, "what did that obscene caller *really* say?"

"Oh, Mom, I don't want to talk about it."

"Come on, tell me."

"Oh, all right." I repeated what he had said.

"What did he mean? Shake *what* thing?"

"Mom! Use your imagination!" Sometimes I think she's as innocent as the kids in her nursery-school class.

You may have noticed that I called Wilma Mom just then. That's because I wanted to seem as innocent as possible so she wouldn't suspect that *I* have obscene thoughts, too.

The fact that I've done a couple of things that I wouldn't want my parents to know about — like smoking dope with Wendy once and watching an R-rated movie on cable TV with Heidi when her parents were out — makes it convenient that they think of me as an innocent little kid.

I'm sure neither of my parents could handle it if I became a Sexy. They think it's perfectly wonderful that I look like a ten-year-old with a couple of pimples. If they had a choice, they would certainly choose to have a smart kid over a sexy one. I mean, let's say I took off for Wendy's party wearing a Paula Proomer–type sweater (first I'd have to get pointier breasts) and green eye shadow — both Wilma and Zeke would probably have heart attacks, and I would be left an orphan at age fourteen. Maybe my parents can be annoying, and they interfere in my life too much. But I wouldn't want them to have heart attacks or anything. I'm really rather fond of them.

Even if they managed to survive after I started looking sexy, sophisticated, like today's woman, and all those other descriptions you see in perfume ads, I shudder to think of the other consequences. I wouldn't want Wilma to see me in high-heeled sandals and leather pants and say to Zeke, "Hey, this kid must have SEX on her mind. She must be smoking dope and watching R-rated movies!" I'd just as soon keep my secrets to myself.

In other words, there are advantages to looking like a Baby. Maybe enough to *keep* me looking like one.

I was so nervous that Wilma would keep bugging me to explain what one's "thing" might be that I brought up the last thing in the world I felt like discussing: the Junior Honor Society.

Wilma went wild with enthusiasm. "That's fantastic, Baby!" she shouted. And dropping her steel-wool scouring pad, she ran out of the trivet-filled kitchen, rousting Zeke from his tête-à-tête with the tube in the living room. "Diana was chosen for the

Junior Honor Society!" she announced, as I trailed in behind her.

Zeke was impressed enough to turn away from the TV and use both hands to push his soft, massive body up off the yellow couch with blue flowers. "That's my girl!" he said. And he spread his arms wide, a signal to start one of my little family's three-way hugs. In other words, I was squashed between the two of them amidst congratulatory squeezes and kisses, virtually smothered with affection.

I decided that I was getting kind of old for three-way hugs. But I didn't think this was the time to put a ban on them.

"You must be excited about the induction assembly," said Wilma. See how well she knows me?

"About as excited as I'd be about the funeral of a close friend," I said.

"Oh, Diana, don't be fresh," said Wilma.

"Maybe I could take off work to come to the assembly!" offered Zeke. "I could rent a video camera, and in years to come we'd have a videotape to —"

"Gee, thanks, Zeke, but I'm sure they discourage parents from coming," I interrupted, trying not to sound panicked. "It will be crowded enough with the whole freshman and sophomore classes in the audience." This subject was getting more and more depressing. But at least Wilma had forgotten about the Obscene Phone Call.

There was an especially exciting basketball development, and Zeke was suddenly reglued to the tube. Wilma headed straight for the kitchen telephone, to inform everyone in Beechurst that *her* Baby was going to be inducted into the Junior Honor Society.

"It's quite an achievement," I heard her say approximately sixty-six times as I finished the dishes.

You see, talking on the phone is Wilma's other main passion besides Garage Sales. When I was a baby, I probably thought the telephone receiver was part of my mommy's body.

Unfortunately, Wilma's favorite topic in her telephone conversations is yours truly. All last summer she boasted via telephone that I was reading a 450-page biography of Mahatma Gandhi in my spare time. I happened to enjoy learning about Gandhi and the nonviolent methods of protest he used in India. But I didn't appreciate her telling everybody on the East Coast about my reading habits.

My whole life is an open book as far as Wilma is concerned. What if things were different, and I was one of the Sexies? Would she be on the phone reporting, "Well, Diana had intercourse again last night"? Somehow I doubt it.

3

I spent most of the next week worrying about the Junior Honor Society induction. Once I was up on that stage, the 442 normal kids in the audience would know for sure that I was smart, boring, and totally unsexy.

The day before the assembly, I felt more nervous than ever. It didn't help that in homeroom Danny Rickovsky said to me, "What are *you* doing in school? I thought you already knew everything there is to know." He gave me one of his dimply smiles, but I couldn't tell whether it was a friendly smile or a sneer. If only he knew that I pay more attention to the way his hair touches the back of his shirt collar than to anything Mr. ("Ass") Aston has to say. But how *could* he know? Sometimes my looking like a ten-year-old comes in handy when it fools my parents and other adults into assuming I have purely innocent thoughts. The problem is that it fools people like Danny Rickovsky, too.

I had to do something to get my mind off the assembly. I decided to go to The Movies after school. There was a late afternoon show of *The Love Nest*, starring Maxine Sanders, at the Beechurst Cinema.

Now, if I could pick my ideal appearance, I would look exactly like Maxine Sanders. Maxine is totally gorgeous. I mean, compared to Maxine, Paula Proomer is homely. I don't think I would have a care in the world if I looked like her. Give me her angular cheekbones, stylish blond hair, turquoise eyes, and perfect body, and I would trade in half my brain and my entire sense of humor.

You should see her costar, Mark Arris! Jet-black eyes you could stare into for hours, perfect-length black hair, and a beautifully muscular body — without looking too scary, if you know what I mean.

I almost invited Wendy to see *The Love Nest* with me. But then I remembered that I'd enjoy it more alone. I don't like any distractions when I go to The Movies. I hate it when someone next to me whispers (like Wendy), "What did he just say?" Or makes a lot of noise eating popcorn (like Zeke). Or gets up to take a leak every half hour (like Heidi — Wendy and I call her the Fountain). Or says (like Wilma), "Oh, I heard about this scene!"

24

The thing is, I don't like to be reminded that it's only a movie. Because for me, The Movie is IT.

Between you and me, when I go to The Movies, I am no longer Diana Pushkin. I become Maxine Sanders or whoever the main female character is. If it's an all-male movie, I'm still the main character. Whoever I am, I am *bigger than life*. I mean I am *dramatic*. Even if the movie is a tragedy and the actress I become has serious problems, well, that's OK. Because my problems are *dramatic*, and *I am a beautiful, sexy-looking woman*. It's the only time in my life I get to feel that way.

So it really depresses me when the lights go on at the end, and there I am, Maxine Sanders, gorgeous and famous, and Wendy or whoever I'm with says, "So, Diana, you wanna get a burger and fries?"

To tell you the truth, I think most people who have been to a movie with me would just as soon have me go alone, too. I can be a little hard to be with. You see, after a movie I usually take on the characteristics of one of the main characters. I may have an English, a French, or a Brooklyn accent. Or I may just stare. I may develop a limp.

Last summer, Heidi and I saw an adventure movie set in London during the nineteenth century. Heidi couldn't handle my acting British afterward at Burger Palace. By the end of the evening she was ready to kill me.

"If you call me Old Chap once more, Diana, it'll

25

be Cheerio to you," she said, wrinkling her nose in freckled disgust.

I finished chewing a french fry that I referred to as a chip, which annoyed her even more. Then I said, "I really cahn't 'elp the way I tsalk, Heidi ol' gull."

Heidi and I exchanged some rather unfriendly words — she in American slang and I in my best Cockney. Then, in our respective accents, we decided never to go to a movie together again.

Luckily, when I watched *The Love Nest,* the theater wasn't crowded. There was no one sitting next to me and fidgeting, talking, coughing, or crunching to remind me it was only a movie, or to keep me from becoming part of it. So by the time I finished my popcorn with extra butter and sucked the shells out of my teeth, I was . . . *Maxine Sanders.*

And boy, did I have troubles in this movie. You see, I had two absolutely gorgeous men in love with me. And I couldn't choose between them because I loved them both. Such a problem.

I couldn't look at Mark Arris or the other male lead (who isn't as famous as Mark Arris but is just as handsome) without having this soft music come on, and without falling into his arms. At the end, the guy who wasn't Mark Arris married a cute-looking waitress and I ended up with Mark, but you could tell that the other guy and I were going to get together once in a while. It was destiny. And chemistry.

Since I was so involved in the movie, I was not at all prepared for the lights to come on after the closing credits. As usual, I sat in my seat longer than anyone else. Then I got up very slowly so I wouldn't break the spell of the movie. I managed to remain Maxine Sanders as I slipped on the bulky orange down parka Wilma talked me into buying, even though it makes me look like a sausage.

In the movie, Maxine had the habit of tossing back her head, which made her wavy blond hair kind of undulate behind her. As I got up to leave, I tossed *my* head, which must have made my cap of brown hair vibrate slightly at its roots. For once I felt sexier than the Sexies. I walked up the aisle, tossing my invisible mane of hair and smiling a close-mouthed, sensual, content, secret smile that meant, "Hey, I know I'm a knockout, and isn't it fabulous? And isn't life a beautiful mystery? But I'm also a soulful, sensitive person, and I feel sad for the poor, non–Mark Arris leading man and all the other unfortunate men who will never enjoy the privilege of having me."

My turquoise eyes watered with sensitivity. I thought I might "go for the record" for remaining a movie character. I was once the British singer-actress Nina Castle for three whole days. By the third day, even Wilma and Zeke were pretty sick of me.

Suddenly, I became aware of an old woman in front of me in the aisle, walking even slower than I was. In my dramatic, dewy-eyed state, I had accidentally mistaken her for empty space and stepped on her heel. I almost turned into clumsy little Diana Pushkin in my embarrassment, but I managed to say, "Oh, please excuse me," in Maxine Sanders's breathy tones and thus retain my identity.

Usually I am not big on making eye contact. You never know what people might discover from looking into your eyes. In school I kind of walk with my head down. And I wear my bangs long (the better to hide behind, my dear!). But after *The Love Nest*, I was Maxine Sanders, and I had nothing to hide. I looked into everyone's eyes with my beautiful, soulful ones. As the matinee crowd trickled out, I hung around the lobby, admiring myself on movie posters. The theater soon emptied because the next show wasn't until later that evening.

Sweeping the lobby was a guy with long, greasy hair, a chain around his neck, and a gray T-shirt with the sleeves rolled up to his shoulders to show off a tattoo of a topless woman. I tossed back my Maxine blond hair and smiled softly at him. Just because he was there.

He turned his broom so the handle looked as if it were sticking out of his crotch. "Hello there!" he said quietly. "The theater is empty. And dark. How about you and me . . . ?"

I was out of there and on the sidewalk before my would-be molester could finish his question. In my panic, I had turned from Maxine Sanders, experienced lover, back into Diana Pushkin, scared-to-death virgin.

I headed for home at a quick pace, still shaking. Not only was I scared, I was furious with myself. There I was, feeling so much like Maxine Sanders that some guy had gotten turned on by my Maxine Sanders smile and sensual eyes in spite of my orange-sausage coat! Maxine would have known what to say to an undesirable sexual partner. But she had disappeared, and I had changed back into a Definitely Not Sexy wimp. No wonder Wilma and Zeke call me Baby.

Now I was confused, too. Was the sweeper just a regular guy, or was he a pervert? Was that how normal men talked if they wanted to have sex with you?

No, the guy was weird, I decided. He had a tattoo, and he had stuck the broom handle out of his crotch, which was not polite at all. I had shown excellent judgment. Maxine Sanders would have run from him, too . . . in fact, I *was* Maxine, and I had run from him.

I was Maxine again!

With my identity reestablished, I managed to get back into my dramatic mood. I tossed back my head as I passed the Beechurst Book Store and smiled sensually as I floated past the Kleen and Dry laundromat and the This-Is-a-Deli and on into my neighborhood.

The naked winter trees had never looked so stunning to me against the darkening blue sky. The small, two-story houses with their wooden porches looked charming and full of emotional appeal. Inside my head, the *Love Nest* theme song played loudly. It was heavy on the string section.

Still Maxine, I sailed up my little driveway, wondering what tender morsels my loving mother was preparing for my evening meal. The frog-sitting-on-a-mushroom sculptures my parents had picked up at a garage sale looked quaint instead of their usual corny.

I walked up the porch steps and knocked on the door in happy anticipation of seeing another leading actress. Instead, a plump, aproned figure who seemed far too unattractive to be Maxine Sanders's mother came to the door.

"Forget your key again? Where in the dickens have you been, Diana?" this strange but somehow familiar woman inquired.

Since for some reason she had called me Diana instead of Maxine, I didn't answer as I floated in.

"Oh, you've been to The Movies," she said. "I can tell by your walk."

I removed my orange parka and sat down at the dining-room table with the sweet, inner smile of a woman who understands the secrets of life.

"Earth to Diana," said the ordinary person masquerading as my mother. "We're eating in the kitchen, not the dining room. The Prince of Wales is not joining us tonight. It's just you, me, and Daddy, eating broiled chicken."

I wandered into a tiny, delicious-smelling kitchen with trivets crowding its walls and sat down next to a person far too rotund to be Maxine Sanders's father.

"So, what movie did you see?" asked the woman piling up my plate with two thighs and a leg, enough chicken to fill out several Maxine Sanderses.

The Love Nest," I said with a sigh.

"Well, I guess we can't stop you from going to movies on weekdays," said the server. "We certainly can't complain about your grades. By the way, how many other kids will be inducted into the Junior Honor Society tomorrow?"

The assembly. I had forgotten about it. *The Love Nest* had taken my mind off it, all right. Now I was filled with dread again. A terrible strangling sound started in my stomach and rose to my throat.

"What's wrong, Diana?" asked Zeke.

"Nothing," I said. But the truth was that *every-*

thing was wrong. The scene I was in would never make it into a movie. The infantile way the main character (me) was being treated, the trivet collection on the walls, the broiled chicken, and especially the talk about the Junior Honor Society had done irreversible damage. I was Diana Pushkin again, and I was not at all happy about it.

4

That night, after Wilma tucked me in (yes, she still does, on the nights when she doesn't fall asleep first), I barely slept. I kept imagining the Junior Honor Society assembly.

Naturally, I was in a terrible mood the next day when it was time to get dressed for the damned thing. Even knowing that I was missing Mrs. Cappell's repulsive French class (Mrs. Cappell speaks French with an Oklahoma accent) did nothing to improve my spirits.

The worse my mood is, the more likely I am to get into a fight with Heidi. Sure enough, backstage, while we were putting on our black cowbell gowns, we argued about everything.

"What do you mean, 'this damned assembly'?"

Heidi said. "You should be proud to be elected to the Junior Honor Society."

"You sound like Wilma," I answered.

"Just think what a good college you'll get into," said Heidi.

"I'd rather be one of the Sexies," I said. "I wouldn't mind skipping college altogether and serving pastrami sandwiches at This-Is-a-Deli if I could be Definitely Sexy and gorgeous."

"I wish you'd appreciate the good stuff about yourself," said Heidi. "So you're not sexy! You're a fine, thinking person, and you'd rather be a shallow person with pointy boobs."

"And have frequent sex," I added.

"Is that all you think about?" Heidi asked, wrinkling her freckled nose. "You're worse than Wendy. At least she's actually had sex, which is more than you can say."

"That's just because I haven't had the opportunity."

"You'd probably run away if you ever did."

That really made me mad. Especially since it might be true. "Hurry out there on stage, Heidi," I said. "Everybody will know for sure you're a Creep. There are so many Creeps in this group, it should be called the Junior Creep Society."

"You're in it, too," said Heidi.

"There are always exceptions," I said. Then I took

comfort in pretending I was in a movie, and I said, "Life is a succession of scenes, some big and some small, but we always see ourselves as the heroes."

"Where did you get that?" asked Heidi, wrinkling her freckled nose again.

"It's from *The Love Nest*. I saw it yesterday."

"Oh. How was it?"

"Great. Maxine Sanders and Mark Arris and this other guy were all totally gorgeous. Mark plays a teacher. I wouldn't mind being in the Junior Honor Society if *he* were the faculty adviser!"

"You have a crush on Mark Arris?!" said Heidi, breaking into her horse's laugh. "Don't get all worked up about him. I read in one of my sister's magazines that he's gay." She guffawed again. Does she ever laugh like a horse!

"You're full of it, Heidi. Mark Arris is *not* gay."

"Sure, sure," she said. And then, Fountain that she is, she headed for the girls' room before the assembly started. I decided that her hair had looked better before Jean-Pierre, the genius, had touched it. It wasn't as curly now, and somehow her chin looked more out of place than ever.

When she came back, she said, "Mark Arris . . . you sure know how to pick 'em, Diana."

I was in no mood for ridicule from a supposed friend. "Go to hell," I said. "You'd probably fit right in there."

But if she was going to hell, I was going with her. . . . The piano music started, which was our cue to grab our as-yet-unlit Candles of Knowledge, stand tall, and march on stage.

There weren't just butterflies in my stomach. There were a couple of large-winged moths and a few wasps, too.

The Junior Creep Society inductees marched on stage — seven freshmen and four sophomores. All smart, unsexy Creeps. And one of us, David Cotter, wasn't even smart. He studies twenty-four hours a day, so he *has* to get good grades. But the guy has zero common sense. We're already in the second semester, and he still can't keep his schedule straight. Sometimes his socks don't match.

You should have seen Ms. Bladadorph, the music teacher, playing the piano. She was so enthusiastic you could puke. She had this mile-wide smile on her face, and her arms, her hands, and even her rear end bounced along with the march music she was pounding out.

When the piano music stopped, we had to stand in a row on stage. We had practiced it all fourteen times. Now there we were at the actual assembly — eleven Creeps in black funeral tents.

We had to stand there while Mr. Altamatto gave a boring speech about how wonderful knowledge is and lots of other hot topics. I spotted Paula Proomer in the third row, and I was especially embarrassed to think that she, looking great in a tight orange sweater, would see me up there like a plastic duck in a shooting arcade, waiting to be blown away.

Mr. Altamatto explained, in more detail than anyone in the audience could ever want to know, why the Junior Creep Society had been founded: "While the Honor Society, for juniors and seniors, has been in existence at Beechurst High for many years, the junior organization was founded just this year —"

— Just to annoy me, I thought. There was adorable Danny Rickovsky on the aisle, toward the back of the auditorium. I was sure he was thinking, What a bunch of dogs up there.

". . . Rote memorization alone does not create learned leaders who will mold future generations . . ." droned Mr. Altamatto.

Hey, David Cotter, you listening to this stuff about rote memorization? I was thinking. Aah, he probably doesn't understand anyway.

". . . Knowledge without true understanding gives but a superficial grasp of the mysteries of science, the wonders of history . . ."

Doug Randow was half watching the proceedings from the sixth row, his eyes half closed as usual. I knew that Diana kid was a loser, he was probably thinking.

"But to learn to think, to question," continued

Mr. Altamatto, "that is THE KEY. All of you can benefit from the examples set by your fellow students of . . ."

I stopped listening. The phrase "that is the key" echoed in my head. Where had I heard that before? *That is the key, the key to my heart* . . . of course, it was from a Julie Paris song, "The Key to My Heart."

Julie Paris is just about my favorite rock star. I've seen her concert movie, *Julie Live!,* three times — twice at a theater and once on Heidi's VCR. I always sing along with her records when Wilma and Zeke waddle off to garage sales on Saturday mornings.

Julie is a terrific singer with this all-male rock band. She wears a leather jacket and leather pants and bright red lipstick, and she clenches the microphone in both hands and sings right into it. When there's a musical interlude, she puts one hand over her eyes and holds the mike by its cord and whips it around in a circle. It's a great act.

If I can't be sexy and gorgeous, like Maxine Sanders, I wouldn't mind being sexy and tough, like Julie Paris. I wouldn't mind at all.

Julie's song kept playing in my head while Mr. Altamatto went on and on, probably putting anybody in the audience who wasn't on speed to sleep. *That is the key, the key to my heart. Your love is the key, don't tear us apart. That is the key* . . .

The plan was that at the end of Mr. Altamatto's speech, all of the Junior Creeps would repeat a totally asinine pledge, and then he would light our candles from his. The Light of Knowledge. Wow. This was the part that called the most attention to us, and I had been especially dreading it.

Mr. Altamatto handed me a candle, but with the music playing in my head and my being up on stage, it didn't seem like a candle. It seemed like a microphone. Julie Paris's microphone. Suddenly, I was no longer a Creep in a black funeral tent. I was Julie Paris in concert.

Mr. Altamatto began the pledge: "I promise to uphold the principles upon which . . . blah blah blah blee . . ."

I repeated what he'd said into my candle microphone, clenching it with both hands like Julie. There were some giggles in the audience, and some murmurs of "microphone." Mr. Altamatto turned around to the Junior Creeps to see what could be causing an audience reaction. I dropped one hand from my candle and transformed myself into plain old Diana Pushkin. Someone in the seventh row with silky blond hair was laughing hysterically. It was Wendy.

My Julie-on-stage act went on for the rest of the pledge. By the Light of Knowledge routine, I was really into it. Mr. Altamatto lit everybody's candle, and Ms. "Enthusiasm" Bladadorph launched into a piano attack. As for me, I was Julie Paris during a musical interlude. And believe me, I've seen her movie enough times to know all her moves. I put one hand over my eyes and whirled the candle around and around.

Heidi, on one side of me, and Billy Munson, on the other, both sidestepped away. I guess they were scared that I would set their gowns on fire.

The audience clapped wildly. Mr. Altamatto, whose back was turned to the row of Junior Creeps, probably thought the applause was for his sleep-inspiring speech and corny lighting ceremony.

At the end of the piano music, I clenched my candle-microphone in both hands, held it way up in the air like a trophy, and bowed my head. Just like Julie Paris. The audience cheered. I heard some shouts of "Go get 'em, Julie!" and "All right, Diana!"

I felt terrific. I had beat the condemnation to Creepdom. I wasn't sentenced to being smart and dull after all. I was smart and funny!

5

"You're crazy, Diana," kids kept telling me at Wendy and her brother Fred's Mother-and-Father-Dear-are-away-for-the-weekend party. I chose to take this as a compliment.

Doug Randow (the druggy guy from my homeroom) started it. "Hey, it's Julie Paris!" he said when I arrived. "I never knew you were such a hot ticket before that assembly!"

"I heard a rumor that you were as high as your grades," said a Moderately Sexy guy named Peter Schultz. "What were you on?"

"Nothing," I said. But I smiled in a spacey way that probably made him figure that not only had I been high at the assembly, but I was high even as we spoke.

I was thrilled that people thought I was doing something not totally goody-goody or even legal for a change. Until the assembly scene, everybody had probably thought I spent all my time studying. I thought it was a riot that I had been dreading the assembly and it had ended up changing my image for the better.

"I think you do downers," said Peter. "You seem pretty out of it."

I could understand why he would say this. I talk slowly just because that's the way I am. And I walk slowly because I'm often thinking about something other than where I'm going. For instance, on my way to English, taught by Mr. Abrams (who is actually Slightly Sexy), I might be imagining I'm Maxine Sanders headed for a rendezvous with Mark Arris.

"*I* think you do *uppers*," said Doug.

Wendy walked over and caught the end of this conversation. She winked at me. She knows I couldn't tell an upper from a downer if I had both in my hand. The truth was that I'd smoked grass only once and certainly hadn't done anything stronger.

Wendy was the one who convinced me to try marijuana. She worships the stuff the way I worship The Movies. I agreed to try it because I wanted to see what it was like, I wanted to think of myself as a person who had tried it, and I wanted other people to think of me as a person who had tried it.

But between you and me, I didn't like it at all. Wendy and I were alone at her house after she got home from camp last August. She was pining for her camp-counselor lover, who lives a thousand miles away, in Florida.

I tried to inhale deeply, the way she showed me. But the smoke burned my throat so much that I kept coughing. I wished the smoke tasted half as sweet as it smelled.

When I finally managed to swallow a few hits, nothing happened. But a little while later, I started laughing like crazy. I laughed so hard my whole body hurt. I felt I would never, could never, stop laughing. It wasn't a pleasant feeling at all.

Meanwhile, Wendy's mood was 100 percent improved, and she was saying, "Well, hey, isn't this stuff extraordinary?"

When I stammered between bouts of hysterics that I thought it was extraordinarily *horrible* and that I felt as if I were stuck on the ceiling, she suggested that I splash cold water on my face. I did, and it helped me come down some.

"Come and sit down with everyone," Wendy said to me, Doug, and Peter.

The music was blasting. I happen to like music

played loud. Whenever Wilma and Zeke go out to a garage sale, I turn the living-room stereo up to full volume. But the music at Wendy's party was a lot louder than I ever played music or would ever want to play music. It rang in my ears and made the top of my head vibrate.

I sat on the floor between Kathy Preston, from my homeroom, and a lamp. Kathy gazed over at me and raised her hand slightly in greeting. I figured the music was too loud for her to bother speaking. At least I didn't have to worry about making conversation.

Doug smoothed his long hair behind his ears, lit up a joint, and started passing it around. I thought how Zeke would die if he saw this scene. He has this thing about cleanliness and germs. For example, he doesn't trust the automatic dishwasher to do a thorough job. He insists that the dishes be washed by hand with soap and hot water *before* they go into the dishwasher. He could never handle the idea of a dozen people putting their lips on the same joint.

Anyway, since I had promised myself not to smoke dope again, I planned to pass the joint right to Kathy Preston when it got to me. I hoped people would think that I had a sore throat or that I was already high from the fourteen other parties I had attended that evening.

Roseanne Capullo took a deep hit and so did Peter

Schultz and Fred, Wendy's brother. Everybody seemed to stare at whoever had the joint.

When it got to Lisa Norris, who was the only other smart, Definitely Not Sexy person there besides me, she started to cough. Wendy got up to bring her a glass of water, which I thought was pretty nice of her since Mark Savage, who she thinks is "extraordinary," had had his arm around Wendy. No one laughed at Lisa or anything. But I was really embarrassed for her.

Suddenly, I knew I wasn't going to have the nerve to refuse that sweet-smelling, burning thing when it was passed to me. I mean, how often do I get invited to a non-Creep party? How often do I get invited to any party? Let's face it, how often do I get out of the house?

Maybe if Heidi had been there to abstain along with me, I would have had the nerve to turn it down. But Heidi was vacationing with her family in the Virgin Islands. (We had made plenty of jokes about the Virgin part before she left. Heidi and I are getting along fine again. Both of us are careful not to mention Mark Arris, though.)

When Sarah Kates passed the joint to me, I put it between my lips and took a drag. I tried to look as if this was something I did every day. I was extremely grateful that I didn't cough or choke or drop a burning ash on my thigh. I tried to pass the joint to Kathy, but her eyes were closed and she was swaying with the music. I nudged her gently with my elbow, but she kept swaying. From the looks of Kathy and some of the other kids, there must have been a few joints going around before I got to the party.

The joint was getting kind of small, and I really wanted to get rid of it before it burned my fingers. I nudged Kathy a little harder while I exhaled the smoke as nonchalantly as I could. Unfortunately, I elbowed old Kathy a little harder than I intended to, and at the same time the smoke I was trying to exhale as slowly as possible exploded right in her face. Kathy ended up coughing and landing on top of Sally Marverstein, who was sitting next to her.

I was slightly mortified. I made up for this rather poor start by taking hits from the next — I don't know how many — joints that came my way. This wasn't like the first time I smoked. I got high right away. When I discovered myself trying to pass a joint to the lamp instead of to Kathy, I considered myself definitely stoned.

My whole body, not just the top of my head, started vibrating with the music. It's hard to explain, but I felt that I had drawn a hot column of pulsing something — electric nervousness, maybe — through the joint and into my body. The nervousness and the music were racing around inside me and glowing and throbbing. The trouble was that I didn't know what to do with this electricity. I would have liked to run or jump or dance, but everybody else was just sitting there. I wished someone would put on a Julie Paris record. Maybe that would inspire people to dance.

Doug kept trying to tell Wendy something, but she couldn't hear him over the pounding music. It sounded as if he were saying, "Waaa, da rara's skaaing." And she would say, "What?" And he would repeat, "Waaa, da rara's skaaing."

Suddenly the music stopped because Sarah Kates took the needle off the record. Wendy's "Whaaat?" echoed strangely through the music-less room.

"The record's skipping!" shouted Doug.

"Oh," said Wendy.

I thought that little conversational exchange in the suddenly silent room was pretty hilarious. And the fact that no one else was laughing or even talking made it seem even funnier to me.

The trapped nervousness in my body started to come out as giggles and then chuckles and then peals and gales and torrents of laughter. And there I was again, stoned and feeling that I could never stop laughing. I hated it. My whole body hurt. It wanted to stop, but it was helpless.

Everybody just sat around, their eyes small red slits with gray rings underneath. These people looked as if they had some disease. And I figured that I must have it too, only I had it worse, because I kept laughing, laughing, laughing. Suddenly, I felt that I might heave up the three portions of spaghetti and meatballs Wilma had encouraged me to eat before the party.

I stumbled my way to the bathroom and remembered Wendy's prescription to counteract the effects of dope: generous amounts of ice-cold water splashed on the face. After dousing myself with enough water to seriously deplete the Atlantic Ocean, I felt less queasy, and I started coming down to earth. With relief, I realized I had actually stopped laughing.

Wendy was waiting for me outside the bathroom. "You OK, Diana?" she asked, her pretty blue eyes puffy slits of concern.

"Yeah. I had to head for the cold water again." I was glad to have Wendy there. I felt that she was an expert on all this and would take care of me.

"Well, hey, want to do some 'ludes?" she asked. "Mark has some. They'll relax you."

"No thanks, Wen." The last thing I wanted was to get *more* stoned. I was thinking that Wendy had an odd way of taking care of me when Mark wandered over. He put his arm around her again, letting his fingers weave themselves through her silky blond hair.

"Hey, Diana," he said. "what *were* you on at that assembly? Doug says speed. I say 'ludes. Am I right?"

"I'll never tell," I said.

Back in the living room, Doug was dancing. You know how most people dance to the rhythm or the bass line of the music? Doug was dancing to the lead guitar — his arms and legs and long hair flying around like the branches of a willow tree on a windy day. Maybe he was trying to get rid of the electric nervousness in his body, the same way I had felt earlier. He was smiling, and he looked as if he thought he was this graceful, even magical, dancer. I always used to think Doug was really cool and interesting because he looked high all the time and as if he had more important things on his mind than his grades or the morning announcements. But to tell you the truth, the way he was dancing, he looked like a marionette whose puppeteer had gone slightly nuts. He looked . . . well . . . ridiculous.

I had been dying to dance before. But I didn't feel like it anymore.

The music wasn't as loud now. Still, no one said much. They sat in separate, toked-up universes. This time I was absolutely positive that I wouldn't do drugs again. Ever.

But I'll tell you what's terrific. With my new image at school, I have the advantage of *seeming* to do drugs without actually doing them. It's the best of both worlds. I'd *much* rather be thought of as crazy, stoned-out Diana than Diana the Creep.

* **6** *

School has been a lot more fun since my status has
risen. I've had the nerve to make more jokes. For
instance, one day in gym class Sally Marverstein
raised her hand and asked Miss Babson why we have
to wear gym uniforms.

"Yeah, they're so ugly and baggy," Paula Proomer
agreed in her husky voice.

"Well, hey, at my cousin's school, you can just
bring in your own shorts to wear," Wendy said.

"How come Beechurst is so old-fashioned?" asked
Lisa Norris.

Before Miss Babson could answer, I yelled out,
"Don't you know? Mr. Altamatto's brother-in-law is
in the uniform business."

My whole gym class cracked up. Even Miss Babson, whose natural facial expression is somewhere between sour and really sour, tittered slightly.

Another day at lunch, Mrs. Randall, the cafeteria aide, was giving us a lengthy tongue-lashing about being disorderly, noisy, and rude. I raised my hand and said, as loud as my peep of a voice would allow, "But haven't you read the study in *Psychology Reports*? Oven-baked chicken three times a week can lead to obstreperous behavior and even juvenile delinquency!"

"Crazy Diana strikes again!" someone shouted.

There was a general increase in disorderliness, noise, and rude laughter, much to Mrs. Randall's dismay.

For days after that, when kids passed me in the hall, they would say, "Oven-baked chicken three times a week!" and laugh.

One morning in February, the P.A. system broke, so the announcements had to be read aloud in each homeroom instead of being blared over the loudspeaker.

"Does one of you ladies and gentlemen want to read these?" asked Mr. ("Ass") Aston. "I seem to have a touch of laryngitis this morning, and I need to save my voice for my chemistry *stew*dents later."

Poor kids, I thought. Then, to my surprise, I

found myself walking to the front of the room to volunteer. I forgot about not liking to talk in front of groups — I couldn't miss such a golden opportunity to make fun of school.

As I looked over the announcements, I pretended I was this crazy newscaster named Nancy Noodlie in the comedy movie *Boogie Time*. I said, "Let's see . . . it says here — wow, listen to this — there will be no school on Fridays, starting this week. And what else? There will be a Mark Arris look-alike contest this afternoon in the Home-Ec Room. And hey, this is wild! Starting next week, anyone arriving late for homeroom will be fined fifty dollars. The second time you're late, you'll be shot! I knew there was a move toward law and order, but this is ridiculous!"

Everybody in my homeroom was really yukking it up. Even Mr. Aston gave a tilted smile, and then he asked me to read the real announcements. Which I did.

When I went back to my seat, Paula Proomer turned around to look at me with her green, eye-linered eyes and said with a laugh, "You're something, Diana. This homeroom would be pretty dull without you."

I was sure Paula still thought of me as a Creep. Perhaps a clever Creep, but a Creep nonetheless.

"The chick's *gotta* be on speed," said Doug Randow, roused from his usual stupor.

I heard a deep voice ask from a couple of rows away, "Who was that? Who just made up those announcements?"

"Diana Pushkin," answered Kathy Preston.

I turned to see who was asking about me. It was a guy I had never seen before.

Maybe you can't fall in love at first sight. But you can sure fall in lust. There in homeroom 9-7, with a bunch of fourteen- and fifteen-year-olds, was this stranger who looked at least nineteen. Even sitting down, he looked taller than everyone else. And his body was very well developed. He had thick blond hair and brown eyes that could look right into you. He had a big nose with lots of character and an inviting smile. I guess I already mentioned his voice. It was at least an octave below the voices of the other mere boys in my homeroom. He was a man!

I was dying to know who he was, when Mr. ("Ass") Aston said, "Oh, I almost forgot. . . . Today we have a new *stew*dent who just moved to Beechurst. James Peterson. James, stand up so we can all see you."

That's the best suggestion Mr. Aston ever made, I thought. Definitely, James, stand up so we can see you.

"What do you like to be called, Mr. Peterson?" asked Mr. Aston.

"Jim is fine, or Jimmy," said James Peterson.

Or Honey or Sweetheart, I thought.

"Well, welcome to Beechurst High!" said Mr.

Aston. "Be sure to get here on time and maintain our alphabetical seating arrangement, and we're sure to get along fine."

Suddenly, I felt religious. Thank you, God, for giving me a last name that begins with P, so I can be in Jimmy Peterson's homeroom, I thought.

When the bell rang I stood up, and I saw Jimmy look in my direction and smile. I was so embarrassed, I tripped over the metal leg of my chair and almost dropped my books. If I had known this hunk was in my homeroom, I never would have had the nerve to make those phony announcements. Then I saw that Jimmy's smile wasn't aimed at me after all. It was directed at Paula Proomer. Of course. Just what she needed, another guy mooning after her. Another guy for the parties I was sure she had. Not boring pot parties like Wendy's. Wild sex parties.

Hey, Paula, I thought. Couldn't you spare just one guy for me? You can keep all the rest, even Danny Rickovsky with dimples and all. But how about letting me have this one? Just one?

Jimmy Peterson was never out of my thoughts for the rest of the day. I floated through my classes as if I had just been to The Movies.

One thing was certain. Now that I'd seen Jimmy, my life would never be the same.

7

Jimmy Peterson has turned out to be an unusual guy. The whole school is talking about him. Not everything being said is complimentary, either. It seems kids either hate him or love him. As for me, the more I hear about and see of him, the crazier I am about him.

First of all, one of the reasons he looks older is that he *is* older. He was left back in third grade in a city public school. I love it — LEFT BACK. No one I hang around with was left back. All the boys in my classes are so smart, you could puke. They're all programmed from birth to go to college. And ever since nursery school, they've known just what they want to be when they grow up — doctors, lawyers, engineers, computer analysts.

Last month, Billy Munson was practically in tears because our biology teacher gave him a lowly B+ for the second marking period. "But Mrs. Axelschmidt," he pleaded. "It lowers my average two tenths of a point! And the average average of students accepted at Eastern Tech is at least a tenth of a point above mine."

Mrs. Axelschmidt was not moved. She said old Billy should have thought about his average when he took the eye of the dogfish he was assigned to dissect and put it in the drinking fountain outside the main office. I felt sorry for Billy because he was so distraught. I asked him why he already had his heart set on Eastern Tech. After all, we're only in ninth grade.

"Eastern Tech has the best aeronautical engineering program around," Billy said sadly. "I've wanted to be an aeronautical engineer for as long as I can remember."

You see what I mean about the species of male in my classes? I didn't have the heart to tell Billy that I don't even know what an aeronautical engineer does or is.

I certainly don't know what I want to be yet. I don't think I want to be anything. I mean, I don't want to be any *one* thing. I certainly wouldn't become a computer analyst, for example, and then just think of myself as a COMPUTER ANALYST, like some of these nerds in dark-colored suits you see getting off the commuter train at Beechurst Station. They look as if they've forgotten their first names.

I think I'd like to be everything there is to be for about two weeks apiece, and then maybe I could choose a couple of the things I liked most. That's one of the best things about going to The Movies — you can become all sorts of different people just by watching. Or at least *I* can.

Anyway, Jimmy Peterson's being left back makes him a welcome change from the college-bound, future bores of America who infest my honors classes.

There is lots of other interesting gossip about Jimmy. He doesn't live with *either* of his parents. They got divorced a few months ago and they live in separate apartments in the city. Since he doesn't get along with either one of them and they both want to live alone for a while to sort things out, Jimmy moved in with his big sister in Beechurst. She's nine years older than he is. And rumor has it that she's plenty wild.

Talk about freedom! Jimmy can do just about anything he wants. He doesn't have to remember not to swear, and he doesn't have to eat healthy foods, or dress in a certain way, or be home at a specified time. He doesn't have to go home at all. He's practically on his own at age fifteen and a half.

Jimmy has a job. He works in the next town at the Lawson College snack bar, clearing tables, sweeping the floor, and doing other stuff like that. I guess you'd call him a busboy. That doesn't sound too exciting, I'll admit. But get this — he meets a lot of college girls that way, and he actually goes out with them. He looks so mature that the girls figure he's a college student too, and he doesn't exactly try to correct their impression.

He makes friends with a lot of the college boys also. He drinks beer with them, and sometimes they let him borrow their cars.

None of the kids I hang out with would have the nerve to do the things Jimmy Peterson does. Not even Wendy, who in summer camp last year used to leave a big doll in her bunk bed and then stay out all night.

I've been having dreams about Jimmy. In one of them, Mrs. Axelschmidt announced that we would have a two-part biology lesson on human reproduction. She explained that in the first part the girls would be impregnated. In the second part, nine months later, our babies would be delivered. Guess who my partner was for this highly educational, highly coeducational experiment? Right! Jimmy Peterson. We had sexual intercourse on one of those hard green lab tables. That part of the dream was pretty fuzzy since, virgin that I am, I have no idea what sexual intercourse is really like.

Then the dream jumped to nine months later. I had a huge belly. And Jimmy asked me if I would marry him after our child was born. Before I could say yes and melt into his arms as in a scene from *The Love Nest*, I woke up. Or rather, I was rudely awakened by someone shaking my shoulder and repeating, "Time to get going, Baby, time to get going, Baby!"

I groaned, hid under the blankets, and pleaded, "Oh, Wilma, let me go back to sleep." I was dying to slip back into my warm dream and find out if Jimmy and I would get married.

"How many times have I asked you to call me Mom, not Wilma? You still sleepy, Baby?"

"Yeah," I whined, falling into my comfortable, Poor Baby role. I wasn't about to let on that I had been dreaming about having sexual intercourse.

"Come on, I'll make you some French toast," said Wilma. "A good breakfast can cure whatever ails you." That's Wilma's lecture 8B. Like most parents, Wilma and Zeke repeat themselves *a lot*. Last fall, when I was stuck in bed with the flu for a week, I assigned classification numbers to Wilma's and Zeke's lectures, just to pass the time. For example, "A cluttered room clutters your thoughts," is Wilma's lecture 9A. "If you have a positive attitude, you're halfway there" is Zeke's 12B.

I vowed to get to know the fascinating Jimmy Peterson. First I had to get up the nerve to talk to him. That had to be the first step toward becoming his lover. I was tired of being the only girl I knew who had never French-kissed. Even Heidi, who thinks it's better to be smart than sexy, had French-kissed with a "sensitive-looking" lifeguard at her parents' pool club one time last summer. I was sure that sex with Jimmy Peterson would be the warm, heavy-on-the-string-section experience I had seen so often in The Movies.

It shouldn't have been hard to talk to Jimmy. He was very friendly. How else could everybody in Beechurst High School know about his exploits at Lawson College?

The trouble was that my high little voice broke and my babyish face caught fire whenever I got close to striking up a conversation with him. One day, I managed to get near him in the hall after homeroom. With my face burning and my heart pounding, I began, "So, Jimmy . . . ," but my voice came out as this tiny croak. He didn't even hear me above the sound of locker doors slamming and kids yelling to each other. He walked on, whistling. He has this terrific bouncing, confident walk.

The next time I tried, I made sure he heard me. I wasn't going to let all my nervousness and perspiration — not to mention the two hours I'd spent planning my outfit — go to waste.

"So, Jimmy, how do you like this place so far?" I asked on our way out of homeroom. My voice cracked, but at least I completed an entire sentence.

"Oh, it's not too bad here," he said, aiming his brown eyes down at me.

"About halfway between gross and putrid, right?" I said, a little softer than the way I had rehearsed it twelve times a morning for the past three days.

It actually worked — Jimmy laughed. "You're the funny one!" he said. "You made those crazy announcements my first day."

"That was me."

"I hear you put on quite a show a couple of months ago at the Junior Honor Society assembly. I'm sorry I missed it."

The rehearsed part of my conversation was finished. So all I could think of to say was "Yeah." I couldn't believe he had spent time listening to gossip about *me*.

"Maybe you could show me your Julie Paris impression in private sometime," he said. And he gave me the sexiest look I had ever seen outside of The Movies. He was talking to me the way Mark Arris might talk to Maxine Sanders!

"I was thinking, Sure, Cutie, anytime. But I was

61

too scared to abandon my usual little-girl image and come on like one of the Sexies. I just giggled and said, "Yeah." And he bounced on ahead.

Now that the ice is broken between Jimmy and me, we talk almost every day between homeroom and first period, when he goes to world history and I go to French in the same direction. It's our only chance to talk. He isn't in any of the honors classes, and we have different lunch periods. On days when he walks out of our homeroom with someone else — Paula Proomer or Cynthia Rosen, or even Danny Rickovsky — I feel jealous and angry and depressed all day.

In those few minutes before first period, I've found out a lot about Jimmy. He seems to love to tell me stories about college girls.

"I went out with a sophomore last night," he said one day.

"How old do these girls think you are?" I asked.

"My story is that I'm nineteen and I'm working my way through acting school in the city," he said. "I tell them I go to classes in the morning and work at the snack bar afternoons."

This was fascinating to me, since I myself hardly ever lie! "And they believe you?" I asked.

"Sure," he said. "They want to. They wouldn't want to admit to themselves that they're attracted to a fifteen-and-a-half-year-old. They might be accused of seducing a minor or something." He gave me one of his sexy looks, and I felt as if I were being filmed in a movie romance. I was the cute female lead being wooed by the lead hunk.

I can't believe I'm making friends with someone so exciting. And he looks at me in a way . . . well, sometimes I could swear he's turned on. Maybe he senses that underneath my crazy, little-girl outside lurks a sensual woman.

Wendy and Heidi are always teasing me about Jimmy, who has replaced movies and who's sexy and who isn't as my favorite topic of conversation. They can't understand what I see in Jimmy.

At lunch, I bore them with every detail of our after-homeroom talk.

"Big deal! He goes out with college girls!" Heidi said one day, between bites of macaroni and cheese. "I wouldn't necessarily believe what he tells you anyway. He lies to his so-called college girlfriends, doesn't he?"

"People have *seen* him driving around with older women," I said. "Besides, he wouldn't lie to me."

"Well, hey, maybe he's riding around with his big sister dressed up in different disguises," said Wendy. She started cackling like a chicken, and Heidi broke into her horse's laugh.

"Jimmy Peterson is much too clumsy-looking to be Definitely or even Moderately Sexy," announced Heidi, really rolling now. "He reminds me of the abominable snowman."

"He's masculine!" I said.

"Keep your shirt on, Diana," said Wendy, playing with the ends of her own smooth blond hair. "If you had more experience with guys, you'd have better taste." Wendy never loses an opportunity to allude to the fact that *she* went all the way with her "extraordinary" camp counselor.

"Jimmy isn't sensitive-looking at all," said Heidi, wrinkling her freckled nose. "*I* go for sensitive-looking guys."

"You mean wimps," I said, stabbing my fork into a canned peach.

"And that nose!" said Heidi. She broke into her neigh again, which prompted Wendy to start her cackle.

"His nose has character," I said.

"It's even longer than Zeke's honker," said Heidi.

"I'd really feel sorry for old Jimmy if he got a cold," said Wendy. She and Heidi got hysterical. They sounded like a whole barnyard.

When they calmed down a little, I said, "You'd feel different if you talked to him."

"Yeah — instead of just disliking him, we'd hate him!" said Wendy. "When you carry on about the wonders of Jimmy 'the Nose' Peterson, I think you really *are* on drugs, Diana." With that, she and Heidi got hysterical again.

When they stopped laughing, Heidi said, "Honestly, Diana, you always sell yourself short — you could do a lot better than Jimmy Peterson."

This conversation was starting to remind me of the fight we'd had about Mark Arris. Only this time there were two against me. To change the subject, I asked Heidi and Wendy if they were going to the exchange-student meeting Friday night. It was for anyone interested in spending a school year in another country.

I would be totally terrified to travel to a strange country by myself, live with a strange family, and go to a strange school for ten whole months. I would be afraid to go to Rosedale — the next town over from Beechurst — for two weeks by myself. Even if I stayed with close relatives.

But as I told Wendy and Heidi, I was planning to go to the information meeting anyway, just to have something to do. It wasn't as if I had any other dates for Friday night. Wendy and Heidi said they figured they would go too, mainly to find out who else was applying to be a foreign-exchange student.

Just then, Paula Proomer walked by with her lunch tray. "Hi, Diana," she said huskily.

"Hi," I answered, pleased to be addressed by a Definitely Sexy in front of my friends.

"Can't you see Paula as a foreign-exchange student?" whispered Heidi. "She'd give some impression of our country!"

"Well, hey, she's had plenty of experience being *a broad*," said Wendy. And she and Heidi started yukking it up again.

I looked at Paula, who was making her way to her seat in a close-fitting red sweater that contrasted beautifully with her jet-black, wavy hair. Her jeans were so tight you could see where her buttocks separated. Then I looked down at *my* clothes — a medium-green cotton turtleneck and a dark-blue corduroy skirt. Baggy and boring. It was Wilma who had talked me into buying the outfit. She said it was practical because the turtleneck would go with pants or a skirt, and the blue corduroy skirt would "go with everything."

Looking at Paula (how could anyone manage to look sexy carrying a macaroni and cheese school lunch?), I was furious with myself for letting Wilma pick out my clothes. Sure, everyone thought I did drugs now, but I still looked like a ten-year-old with a couple of pimples. How could I expect Jimmy to be interested in me if I looked so uninteresting?

I had to do *something* to change my little-girl image once and for all.

8

Just about all the Sexies wear *gobs* of makeup. So I decided to start enhancing the less-than-glamorous face I've been blessed with.

The foreign-exchange-student meeting presented a golden opportunity for my makeup debut. My parents were going out to dinner that night with the Martins, friends of theirs who are so dull they make Wilma and Zeke seem positively wild.

They took their time getting ready. Wilma was nervous about leaving her Baby. She asked me four times if I was sure Heidi's mother would be picking me up soon. Twice she gave me her lecture 28B: "Don't open the door unless you're sure who's on the other side!"

"OK, Mom," I said in my best Baby voice, so she

wouldn't suspect I was about to undergo a physical transformation.

Zeke was all grumbly about having to go out when this great boxing match was on TV. Wilma practically had to start a boxing match with *him* to pull him off the yellow couch with blue flowers and get his sports jacket on him.

Before they left, they just about forced me into one of their three-way hugs. I am definitely getting too old for those.

When they finally lumbered out, I rushed to their bathroom in search of makeup. Look out, Beechurst, Diana Pushkin was about to become Maxine Sanders.

Wilma, as a rule, doesn't wear makeup, except for pink lipstick. But I knew she had some in her medicine cabinet that had been "marked down to almost nothing" at a garage sale. Whenever Wilma buys something at a garage sale that deep down inside she knows she won't use, she says, "You can never tell when you might need it" (Wilma's lecture 17A). This time, she was right.

From the depths of the medicine cabinet I excavated lipstick, mascara, eyeliner, and rouge. I laid it out on the sink and stared at it. Suddenly, I was more in awe than ever of Paula Proomer and the other Sexies. They had to be smarter than they seemed. The hotshot honor student (me) hadn't the faintest idea of how to use this stuff.

First I smushed on some rouge. Too much — I

looked like a clown. Then I couldn't manage to confine the lipstick exactly to my lips, so I looked as if I had a pink mustache.

Now it was time for the eye makeup. I combed my long bangs out of my eyes to get ready. But the eyeliner was a *total* mystery to me — how can you see where you're applying it when you need to keep your eyelids closed in order to put it on? As for the mascara, more of it ended up on my cheeks and forehead than on my eyelashes.

Staring in the mirror at my experiment in image improvement, I gave myself a D−, far below my usual honors grades. I looked like a clown who had been beaten up and sent out into a rainstorm.

Soap and water washed most of the mess off my face. Then I started again. This time I put on much less of everything. I managed to keep most of the stuff on the places where it was supposed to go, except for the eyeliner, which was halfway up my lids. It was a very faint line, I reassured myself.

Studying myself in the mirror, I decided that I no longer looked like a clown. But now it was hard to tell I was wearing makeup at all. I was disappointed to see that I didn't bear the slightest resemblance to Maxine Sanders.

There was no time to start over. Wilma and Zeke had taken so long getting out of the house that Heidi and her mother would be picking me up any minute. I tried to cheer myself up with the thought that I embodied the famous and desirable Natural Look.

When Heidi's mother honked, I dashed out to the car and got into the backseat next to Heidi.

"How do I look?" I asked.

"Fine," Heidi said. "I don't know why you think you look like a sausage in that orange parka."

"No, look at my face," I whispered.

"I can't see, it's dark," she said.

"I'm wearing makeup."

"What's the occasion?"

"I'm just tired of looking like a ten-year-old."

"I wish you wouldn't be down on yourself all the time. You're really kind of nice-looking. And you're a good person, which is more important than — Wait a minute, does this have anything to do with that asshole?"

"Heidi, would you watch your language?" said Mrs. Kellermeier. "If I'm going to be your personal chauffeur, the least you can do is not talk like a longshoreman."

"Oh, Ma," said Heidi.

"Does this have to do with *what* asshole?" I asked. "Oops, sorry, Mrs. K."

"Jimmy Peterson."

"Maybe."

In the cafeteria there were folding metal chairs set up for the meeting. The big room seemed strangely quiet in the evening, without its usual clatter of plates and utensils, kids shouting from one table to another, and Mrs. Randall, the cafeteria aide, shouting at kids to stop shouting.

Heidi and I found seats near the back. The head of the exchange program, Lisa Norris's mother, stepped up to the podium to introduce a nerd who had been to Spain the year before, when he was a junior. The nerd talked about his never-to-be-forgotten experiences living in a different culture. The guy was BORRRRRRRing. He made Mrs. Cappell, my French teacher, seem fascinating in comparison.

Just as I thought he was about to wrap things up, he whipped out some slides and bored us for another twenty minutes. He said things like "It's too bad the color got a little washed out on this one" and "You see that tiny speck in the upper right-hand corner? That's a rare bird we saw while we were hiking."

I couldn't wait for the speeches to end so I could walk around and have everybody check out my makeup. I was sorry that Jimmy, the main reason for my wanting to change my Definitely Not Sexy image, wasn't there. He wasn't exactly foreign-exchange-student material. Besides, he was probably having passionate sex with some college girl at that very moment, while I was stuck listening to this nerd-bore!

After the nerd finally finished talking, Mr. Abrams, my Slightly Sexy English teacher, gave a speech about how wonderful it is to have a foreign student stay in your house. The idea of being a host to some Creep from another country appeals to me almost as much as the thought of being a Creep in a foreign country myself.

Finally, we were told to get up and help ourselves to refreshments and application forms. All right! I thought. Mingling time! Heidi, the Fountain, immediately headed for the girls' room. I noticed that Jean-Pierre, her genius hairdresser, hadn't had his paws on her curly red hair lately, and she looked 100 percent better. Her oversized chin wasn't nearly as noticeable.

As I started wandering around, I was so aware of wearing makeup that I felt like a movie star. No one else seemed to notice the New Me, though. I waited for someone to say, "Diana, you look fabulous!" or "You look older somehow — what have you done to yourself?" But all I heard were a bunch of giggles and "stoned again"s. I decided that my new stoned-out image might have turned off these foreign-exchange-student/honors-Creep types. No one spoke to me.

"What is all this talk about foreign-exchange students?" I finally asked a clump of kids. "I thought there was supposed to be a heavy metal concert here tonight." The clump laughed in kind of an embarrassed way. I had the distinct impression that they were avoiding looking at me. These honors types couldn't handle my new, more sophisticated appearance. That was it! Not just the drug stuff.

Finally, Lisa Norris asked me whether I was applying to be a foreign exchange student.

"No way, José, not a prayer, Pierre. You catch my drift?" I answered.

"I bet you'd love to be placed in South America and get hold of some Colombian grass!" said Richie Kessler. The clump laughed a lot harder then I felt was called for. And I could swear they all directed their gazes at the speckled beige cafeteria linoleum instead of at my new, cosmetically improved visage.

When my English teacher walked by, I called out, "Hi, Mr. Abrams!"

"Good evening, Diana," he said with an odd smile, and he started to move on. But I wouldn't let him. My new image was wasted on my peers. I would try it out on a worldly, mature man.

"You must really like this school!" I said to Mr. Abrams, so he would have to keep talking to me or seem totally rude. "You're here day and night!"

"It seems that way," he said, looking ill at ease. Was he attracted to me? He already respected my mind (that was definitely a plus about my being smart) — I could tell from his comments on my English papers. And now that I looked so much more grown up, who knew what might happen between us?

"Well, I have to speak to Mrs. Norris about something," said Mr. Abrams. "Take care of yourself, Diana," he said in a very serious manner. He walked away, shaking his head.

Perhaps he sees something in me he's never seen before, I thought.

I was trying to figure out exactly how many years older than fourteen Mr. Abrams was when Heidi finally emerged from the girls' room.

"So, Heidi," I said, "we're not in the dark car now. Can you see my makeup?"

"I can see it all right," she said in the same kind of superior tone she had employed to inform me that Mark Arris was gay and that Jimmy Peterson was a clumsy-looking liar with a big nose. "I wish you would realize that you're a really neat person. You don't have to start wearing makeup and —"

I had heard Heidi's "Appreciate yourself" rap often enough to know it by heart. She repeats herself so much that I'm tempted to assign classification numbers to *her* lectures. I interrupted her with, "I decided not to put on too much. I went for the Natural Look. But no one's commented or anything, and people have been acting kind of strange."

"Well, you don't see black cheeks on a Caucasian every day," said Heidi, sounding more superior than ever. "Or red ears."

I rushed to the girls' room. Heidi wasn't kidding. I must have forgotten that I was wearing makeup and rubbed the hell out of my eyes during the boring speeches. There were huge black smudges on my cheeks, my chin, and even my neck. Combined with the rouge, which was no longer confined to my cheeks but had somehow made its way to my nose and ears, I looked as if I had been in a brawl in a coal mine.

I couldn't believe that I had been out there in the cafeteria like that, making conversation with people. No wonder kids had been muttering "Stoned again" and trying not to look at me. I didn't want to look at me, either.

And Mr. Abrams, the only teacher at Beechurst High who is even remotely sexy, had seen me looking like a weirdo. I had imagined he had "seen something in me he'd never seen before." He'd seen something, all right — he'd seen that I'm a total jerk. I wondered if the expression "die of embarrassment" had any literal truth to it.

To clean my face, I used some of that nauseating-smelling school soap you pump out of hanging metal dispensers and, from another metal dispenser, a paper towel that looked and smelled like sandpaper.

The makeup came off OK, but my cheeks were still red from 100-percent-natural humiliation.

Maybe makeup isn't for me, I decided. How did the Sexies I thought were so dumb remember not to rub their eyes? It was a mystery to me.

When I emerged makeup-free and putrid-smelling from the girls' room, I tried to avoid making eye contact with anyone in the cafeteria. Luckily, I ran into good old Wendy, who had arrived too late for the speeches but was loading up on chocolate-chip cookies at the refreshment table.

Now here was someone who really *was* "stoned again." I thought that Wendy ought to cut down on dope. Sometimes she seemed really "out of it." But even with her eyes red from dope smoking, she looked great. Thanks to her tall, slender figure and silky blond hair, *Wendy* doesn't need to wear makeup.

"I'm seriously considering applying to be an exchange student," she said very slowly, with a spacey grin. "I've heard some very inter . . . inter . . . interesting things about foreign men."

We both started laughing. Then we talked about which foreign movie actors we like most. I tried to put the makeup fiasco out of my mind. But it was hard to do. On Monday I would have to face Mr. Abrams in English class. I felt like going through the rest of my high-school career with a paper bag over my head.

∗9∗

The next day was Saturday, which meant I had the morning to myself while Wilma and Zeke combed garage sales. I tried to cheer myself up by singing along with the stereo. I propped up record-album covers on the couch so I would have an "audience" of rock stars to sing to. Before long I was Julie Paris in concert, and the foreign-exchange-student meeting was erased from my mind. (My Julie Paris impression was getting to be pretty impressive.)

Wilma and Zeke's arrival ended my concert, of course. They had purchased *another* trivet, as well as a candy thermometer Wilma claimed would be indispensable someday if she decided to make her own candy. Then they said they had a surprise for *me*. From behind his back Zeke whipped out . . . a big stuffed monkey. It was bright red and cute, but really, a stuffed animal? They must think I'm even younger than I look!

I still thought it might come in handy for them to think of me as Baby. So I said, "Thanks, Mom and Dad. I don't have any stuffed monkeys."

During the last few weeks, I've gotten to know Jimmy Peterson better and better. Besides talking with him after homeroom, I usually hang out with him for a little while after school, too. It's a lucky coincidence that the stop where he catches the bus to Lawson College is on my walk home.

I always put on my jacket in record time so I can make sure to "happen" to walk by the bus stop before his bus comes. Thank goodness, now that it's April, I don't have to wear my orange-sausage parka. I had talked Wilma into letting me buy a denim jacket for the spring. She wanted me to get a creepy red waterproof one.

As for my other image-improvement plans, I gave up makeup after the exchange-student/smudged-face incident. But I *have* taken to wearing sunglasses. They're much easier to put on than makeup, and they make me look mysterious. I'm hoping people will give me the benefit of the doubt and assume that an interesting person is hidden underneath.

The only trouble with wearing sunglasses in school is that in some of the more poorly lit corridors I tend to bump into lockers and other students. But I've never seriously injured anyone, and stumbling a little probably adds to my spaced-out image.

Jimmy has been telling me loads of details about his exploits. He's going out with *two* college girls now, and neither knows about the other. Sometimes he shows up in homeroom wearing the same clothes two days in a row, and he confides to me that he hasn't slept at home. Does that make my fantasies go wild! I have never even seen a photo of Jimmy's college girlfriends, but I'm insanely jealous of them. Luckily for me, he's never dated anyone from Beechurst High.

Jimmy says lots of stuff to me that none of the creepy boys in my honors classes would ever say. For instance, when I wear my brown leather boots, he comments in his deep voice, "Pretty foxy, Diana." And sometimes he touches my hair in a gentle way and says, "So soft." It drives me crazy. I've been hoping he can see through my Baby image and is getting ready to ask me out. He certainly seems to enjoy talking to me.

The day after spring vacation, Jimmy bounced up to me after homeroom with a devilish look in his eyes. He pulled out his wallet and handed me a driver's license that said "James Peterson." According to the date of birth, he was nineteen.

"Where did you get this?" I asked.

"One of my college chicks is majoring in graphic arts, and she phonied it up for me," he said proudly. "I told her I lost my old one and I didn't feel like waiting in line for six hours at the motor vehicle bureau to get a new one."

"It certainly looks real," I said.

"Yeah, she's pretty talented," he said, and he ran his tongue across his lips. I was glad I was wearing sunglasses so he couldn't tell how turned on and embarrassed I was.

"Speaking of looking real," Jimmy said, "how would you like to go for a spin in a real car?"

"What do you mean?" I said. Was he asking me out?

"One of my college buddies went to Florida for a couple of weeks. And he lent me this unbelievable sports car. Want me to swing by your house and show it to you tonight?"

"Tonight?" I tried to sound casual even though my body was displaying at least three of the warning signals for heart attacks that we had had to memorize in health class.

"See you around seven," he said. "And don't worry, I'm a great driver."

I was sure he was great at everything.

I wanted to be finished eating dinner, cleaned up, and changed by seven. Naturally, just that night Zeke decided to be talkative. He was all agitated about some basketball player getting busted for possession of cocaine. The guy was on Zeke's favorite team, and he was suspended because of this drug thing.

"It's disgusting," Zeke said. "He ought to be kicked out indefinitely — not just suspended. These teams are far too lenient."

I was wondering what Zeke would think if he knew his Baby was known as the drug queen of the honors crowd.

"But Zeke, dear," said Wilma, "the case hasn't come to trial yet. You're not giving him a chance."

"An athlete in his position should be an example to youth," said Zeke, waving a roast chicken leg to emphasize his point. "And believe me, the evidence was plenty damning — I mean, convincing. Excuse my language, Diana." Zeke's forehead turned red.

"Hot damn, Zeke, that's OK," I said.

"Don't be fresh, Diana," said Wilma. "You kids!" she added, as if my behavior were just a symptom of some dreaded disease called adolescence.

By the time Zeke had finished carrying on about the evils of mixing sports and drugs and about how things sure were different from when he was a kid

(Zeke's lecture 14A), and by the time he and Wilma had polished off the whole roast chicken, a bowl of mashed potatoes, a salad, half a loaf of bread, and a quart of diet soda, it was 6:45.

Luckily, they were too busy talking to notice that I was as jumpy as a cat and I had eaten only a couple of bites of my dinner. I was glad to be spared Wilma's lecture 6B — "You must eat plenty of nutritious food to be healthy and strong and avoid colds, flu, and irregular bowel habits." The fact that she and Zeke have such good nutrition that they look like a mountain range when they stand next to each other is never mentioned.

I whizzed through my kitchen cleanup duties like someone trying out for the Olympic Kitchen Cleanup team. Then I headed up to my room to change. I put on my tightest pair of jeans, which are baggy compared to Paula Proomer's, and a torn black sweatshirt that I think is kind of sexy. I brushed and flossed my teeth, gargled with mouthwash, and combed my cap of hair approximately four thousand times, trying to make it look something other than short, straight, and dull (which, come to think of it, might be a description of me in general).

Adding my sunglasses as the final touch, I stationed myself upstairs at the guest-room window to be on the lookout for Jimmy. It was 7:05. My stomach was having a heart attack. (Is that possible?) I stared at the Matthewsons' pink house across the street. Pink is a nice enough color for a shirt or a facial tissue, but for a house? Yecch.

At 7:15, I decided that Jimmy might have had to work a little late at the snack bar.

At 7:30, I thought he might have gotten lost. He had never been to my house before.

At 7:40, I decided he could have gotten lost, driven around Beechurst six times, and still have made it to my house by then. Maybe he had forgotten.

At 7:50, still perched by the window, I had the terrible thought that he had been in a car accident. Maybe he looked like nineteen, but he was only fifteen and a half, and too young to drive. He might have been drinking, too.

At 7:55, I relaxed about the accident, because I believe that things like that don't happen when you're expecting them to. It would have been too much of a coincidence for me to be worrying about a car accident at the same time he was in one. If you know what I mean.

At 8:00, I faced the fact that Jimmy wasn't coming. The realization made me feel as if someone had kicked me in the stomach. He probably had something more important to do than hanging around with a little Creep like me.

I took off my torn sweatshirt and semitight jeans,

changed into a nightgown, and sat down with my algebra homework at the wooden desk Zeke had built for me the year I turned ten. This was the first time all year that I hadn't knocked off my homework during study hall. I had been too excited about my "date" with Jimmy to concentrate. Now I tried not to drip tears on my final copy.

The next morning after homeroom, Jimmy was friendly, as usual. "Hi, Babes," he said.

"What happened last night?" I asked, trying to sound merely curious instead of deranged with disappointment.

"What do you mean?"

"You were going to show me your friend's car."

"Oh, Diana, I forgot all about it. Hey, I'm sorry. I'll catch you tonight. OK?"

"Tonight? Let me think if I'm doing something. . . . No, tonight is OK."

After school, I tried to "happen" to run into him at his bus stop to remind him about our "date." But then I remembered he wouldn't be taking the bus, because he had his friend's car.

At 7:00 that night, I was at the guest-room window again in my black sweatshirt, jeans, and sunglasses, staring at the Matthewsons' pink house. I wondered whether it would be safe for Jimmy to drive with his arm around me. Every time I heard a car motor, my stomach revved up.

At 7:45, I was taking off my costume and trying to figure out if I was more depressed than angry or more angry than depressed.

The following morning, Jimmy seemed to remember our broken date as soon as he saw me. "Diana, Babes, I'm really sorry. Something came up. I'll definitely swing by tonight. Seven sharp. Elm Street, right?"

That night, at five minutes before seven, just as I had finished changing into my sweatshirt and jeans, which were beginning to feel like a uniform, I heard a car horn. I threw on my denim jacket and ran downstairs past Zeke, who was planted in front of "Great Moments in the History of Basketball" on the tube, and past Wilma, who was firing out questions like a machine gun: "Where are you going? Who's out there? You have a million nice blouses and you have to wear that torn sweatshirt? You kids —"

I forced myself to walk, not run, down the porch steps and out to the driveway. Jimmy stepped out of the car, looking really built in a brown leather aviator jacket. Right away I flashed to this hoody movie I had seen, called *Young and Angry*. He and I were the passionate, rebellious, teenage-lover stars. I was Rhonda. He was Chet.

"What do you think?" he asked, nodding toward the car. It was blue, cute, some kind of sports car. I know zero about cars.

"Nice," I said, barking out the word coldly like Rhonda.

"Reeeeal nice," he said, imitating Chet without knowing it. "Get in."

I did. As Wilma waddled out onto the front porch, Jimmy started the engine with a *varoom*, threw the car into reverse, and backed out of our little driveway. Across the street, Mr. Matthewson peered out of one of his pink-framed windows. I was glad to give him and Wilma something to wonder about for a change.

Where would Jimmy take me? I was dying to know. Heidi had told me the Sexies go to the parking lot at the duck pond to make out. Would I have something to tell her and Wendy in the cafeteria the next day if Jimmy took me there!

Jimmy was too busy revving the engine and showing me how well the car took corners to put his arm around me. "Check out the four-speaker stereo system," he said, and blasted it.

After careening around the narrow streets of my neighborhood for about ten minutes, he parked the car. I was thinking that Maple Street was a strange make-out spot when he started pointing out all the features that made the car such a big deal: reclining seats, padded dashboard, a shelf in the front that could hold a six-pack, lamb's-wool cover on the driver's seat, mirrors under both visors . . .

"Neat," I said.

Suddenly he revved up the engine again. He raced back to my house and squealed up the driveway, stopping just short of the garage door. The frog-sitting-on-a-mushroom sculptures seemed to quiver on our little lawn.

Wilma immediately reappeared on the front porch. "Diana, what are you doing?" she yelled above the blare of the four-speaker stereo system. "Are you all right?"

"I'm fine. It's just a friend of mine from school," I shouted out the window, instantly demoted from Rhonda, Hood Movie Star, to Baby. I couldn't help but feel Wilma's concern was touching, even though it *was* annoying.

"Your mother's quite the wide load," Jimmy said, laughing.

I didn't say anything. It's OK for *me* to criticize old Wilma. But I don't like anyone else doing it.

"Well, I gotta run. Heavy date tonight," said Jimmy, grinning and tapping the leather-covered steering wheel impatiently.

Before I knew it, I was whining, "I thought *I* was your heavy date tonight."

Jimmy burst out laughing. "You?" he said. "Little

Diana? Come on, I go out with college girls, college *women*! You — you're a kid!"

"Thanks for the ride," I said. I got out and slammed the door. It felt pretty tinny for such a big-deal sports car.

I wondered *when* I would find someone to treat me like a woman.

As if I didn't feel disgusting enough, Wilma had to say, as I rushed past her up to my room, "The wrong crowd can be a young person's undoing" (Wilma's lecture 19A).

* **10** *

I haven't allowed myself to sulk about my non-date with Jimmy. "OK, Diana," I told myself, "now that you know where you stand with the guy, maybe you can use your so-called Junior Honor Society brain and think of a way to change things."

My makeup scheme certainly backfired (right in my face — ha ha). And my sunglasses haven't made much of an impression on Jimmy. But I've launched a new campaign to change his attitude toward me. . . .

In homeroom, I make a point of talking to other boys so Jimmy will see me as desired by the opposite sex. I bought this perfume called Irresistible in an attempt to become what it says. And I try to have a sexy gleam in my eye, like Paula Proomer or Maxine Sanders.

I've even started making sexy comments. It isn't easy for me because I'm not used to it. And don't think I'm nuts, but I have this weird feeling that Wilma and Zeke can hear me, even though they're miles away — Zeke selling life insurance in the city and Wilma teaching nursery-school kids, probably about garage sales (just kidding).

One day Jimmy wore a blue shirt with the top two buttons open.

"Why don't you open some more buttons?" I forced myself to comment after homeroom.

"What?" was his response.

"Why don't you open some more buttons?" I repeated, a little louder.

"What for?" he asked.

"So I can see more of you," I said, trying not to grin my Baby grin and trying to deepen my voice a couple of octaves.

Jimmy did not react the way I had imagined he would. He laughed. Then he completely changed the subject. He started talking about this new sports car that had just come out, and how he had a little business deal going at the college, and if things worked out, maybe he could buy himself a sports car by the time he was old enough to get a non-phony driver's license.

That night, I had a dream in which Jimmy and I were lying in the warm sand, rubbing suntan lotion on each other's bodies. It was wonderful. The next day I got up the nerve to tell him I'd been having dreams about him. I didn't go into the details.

"Oh yeah?" he asked in his deep voice. He raised an eyebrow in a sexy way.

"You were pretty good," I said.

"How would you like to make your dreams come true, Babes?" he asked, leaning way down to put his arm around me. Then suddenly he said, "Hey, what am I talking about?" He jerked away his arm, which had just started to feel heavenly. "Will you stop talking like that, Diana? Goddamn it! You make me forget you're just a kid."

"I'm almost as old as you," I said, trying not to whine.

"Not in terms of experience."

"Well, how am I going to get any experience, BABES, if you and everybody else treat me like a goddamned baby?"

"You'd better shut up before you get yourself in trouble."

"That's my business."

"Will you quit talking like some . . . tough chick?" His brown eyes flashed with anger.

Richie Kessler had to pick just that moment to duck his head out of his locker and yell, "Diana, did you finish your world history paper? It's due today!"

"I handed it in last week," I barked back.

Jimmy started laughing. "I guess you really are a *fast* chick," he said.

"Very funny," I said.

Well, I've given up my sexy-comments plan. All it did was get Jimmy angry. He hasn't seemed to notice my talking to other boys, either. And as for the "Irresistible" perfume, I would try to get my money back if I hadn't used up half the bottle already.

At least Jimmy is still talking to me. He doesn't seem to think of me as an honors Creep. In fact, he makes a point of waiting for me in the crowded hall after homeroom. And now *he* looks for *me* after school so we can walk to his bus stop together. (His college friend with the sports car is back from Florida, which means Jimmy is back on the bus.)

Jimmy seems to love to tell me all the wild things he's been doing. Cutting classes right and left. Staying out all night at parties at Lawson College. Telling one of his girlfriends that his grandfather (who passed away before Jimmy was born) had died suddenly the night before, so she would be especially "affectionate."

The "affectionate" story really drove me crazy. But usually I love to hear about his exploits. I mean, the wildest thing an honors Creep like Richie Kessler has ever done is turn in his health homework a day late. And ever since Billy Munson got a lowly B+ in biology after the dogfish-eye-in-the-water-fountain incident, he's been straight as an arrow.

Jimmy is no honors Creep. And strange as it seems, he thinks of *me* as a friend. I suppose I should be satisfied with that. But I can't seem to stop my brain from conjuring up new plans to make him think of me as *more* than a friend.

Last week, which was the last week in May, Jimmy's reputation at Beechurst High hit an all-time low. Now the kids who already hated him hate him even more. Even the kids who used to look up to him hate him now.

On Monday, Jimmy didn't come to school. Tuesday he arrived in really rough shape. I mean, he looked worse than I did on the night of my makeup experiment. He had a black eye, and under it a puffed-out cheek that was black, blue, and red and a bandage on his honker of a nose. (OK, I admit it — it's a honker. But it *does* have character.) He limped and winced his way into homeroom.

"I wonder what happened to poor Jimmy," Paula Proomer whispered to me. I could never understand why someone as sexy and popular as Paula Proomer was always talking to little old yours truly. Our homeroom has plenty of kids "more in her league" for her to talk to.

Everybody was whispering and asking Jimmy if he had been in a fight or an accident or what.

"Keep it down, *stew*dents!" said Mr. ("Ass") Aston.

"I had a run-in with some dudes," was all Jimmy would say.

During our after-homeroom chat, he said, "Let's just say I won't be getting a sports car for a while." His slow limp was in sad contrast to his usual bouncing, confident walk.

"Your 'business deal' fell through?" I asked.

"You got it."

"Want to talk about it?"

"A couple of guys jumped me. Let's leave it at that."

I got the story later. Tommy Massato, in tenth grade, has a brother at Lawson College. The brother told Tommy about it, and by the end of the day it was all over school.

Apparently, Jimmy's "business" was dealing. In between sweeping up and clearing tables at the college snack bar, he would approach students and tell them he had some great grass. Cheap. He made sure to ask kids who looked innocent, as if they hadn't done drugs before.

Then, if they were interested, he would meet them somewhere and sell them plastic bags of grass for a lot of money. If kids complained that they weren't getting high, Jimmy would tell them that that often happened the first few times, and that they ought to keep smoking.

"Hey, they won't let you graduate if you don't get high at least once," he would tell them with a friendly pat on the back.

So the kids would buy more. If they complained again, Jimmy would say that it was too bad and he couldn't understand why they weren't getting high on such great stuff, and then he would say he didn't have any more to sell. He was making a nice little income when one of his buyers shared his stash with a more experienced student, who figured out that Jimmy's "grass" was about one quarter green grass like you grow in your yard, one quarter parsley, and one half oregano.

Everybody at Lawson College who heard what Jimmy was up to is furious with him. Word also got out that he's just a freshman in high school, and *both* his girlfriends broke up with him. He no longer gets invitations to college parties or offers to lend him cars. He was fired from the snack bar.

The kids at Beechurst High think Jimmy Peterson is the lowest of lows for selling phony drugs. I must be the only one who still likes him. "Likes him"? I'm still crazy about him. He could keep me waiting at my guest-room window every night for a month, treat me like a baby, deal phony drugs, and maybe even hold up a bank, and I would still be crazy about him.

Jimmy has such chutzpah! He isn't like anyone I have ever known. And what's so terrible about selling lawn seeds and a couple of spices? They aren't poison. Oregano and parsley are probably far better for you than marijuana.

I'm starting to think that drugs are really bad news anyway. I can't be the only one to have coughing fits and then get scared I'll never stop laughing after smoking grass. Lots of kids have had worse experiences than that. Peter Schultz, who was at Wendy's dope-smoking party last winter, was rushed to the hospital a couple of weeks ago when he overdosed on downers. And Mark Savage, the guy who had his arm around Wendy at the party, has smoked so much dope that he looks as if half his brain is dead. Even Wendy doesn't think he's "extraordinary" anymore. She thinks he's pretty much a zombie.

The more I think about it, the more I think Jimmy did those naive college students a favor. Yeah! He showed them it doesn't pay to buy drugs. Someday, when a dealer approaches those kids with real dope, you can bet they won't be so quick to buy it. They'll probably turn around and run!

I may be the only one who looks at the Jimmy

situation this way, but I think he's sort of a hero. And I can't help feeling that Jimmy is even more exciting for being a hero and a criminal at the same time.

I picture the two of us as tragic lovers in The Movies. I send him erotic letters in jail and talk to him through the visitor's grate. He's a handsome prisoner convicted of a crime that's not really a crime. And I am loyal, brave, and beautiful — the heroine of a movie set in Georgia, standing by my man. I even bring him my own secret-recipe fried chicken when I'm allowed to visit. And just as the judge is about to sentence old Jimmy to twenty long years in the slammer, a telegram arrives from the President of the USA: "SET THIS MAN FREE. STOP."

The scene switches, and Jimmy and I are at the White House in the Oval Office or the octagonal room or some other weird-shaped room, and the President's wife pins a medal of honor on my Jimmy. He is a soldier in the war against drugs.

Let's face it. Jimmy Peterson would have to do a lot worse than rip off some dumb college kids to turn *me* off.

11

One Friday night in June, Lisa Norris had a party. I wasn't particularly looking forward to it. Lisa is nice enough, but she is, after all, an honors Creep. And Heidi and I had decided that just about everyone invited was either a Not Sexy or a Definitely Not Sexy.

Just to practice changing my image, though, I wore my tightest T-shirt and white jeans like the ones Maxine Sanders had on in the walking-along-the-beach scene in *The Love Nest*. Naturally, since I had a party to go to for a change, a huge pimple made its appearance on my chin. And naturally, while Wilma drove me to Lisa's, I had to listen to "You have such lovely dresses and you go to a party looking like a slob. And I *wish* you would cut those bangs. You kids! I don't understand why sloppiness is the goal of your whole generation." (The last part is Wilma's lecture 9B.)

It was a warm night, and the party was in the backyard. The stereo speakers were aimed out onto the patio. It was neat to be outside at night with rock music playing, even if I had to be surrounded by Creeps. Lisa's parents were kind enough to remain out of sight somewhere in the house.

There were some great-looking dips and chips set out on little plastic snack tables. Wilma has dozens of those tables from garage-sale expeditions. She uses them about once every three years, but of course she says, "You can never tell when you might need them" (Wilma's lecture 17A).

Anyway, I was too concerned about spilling food on myself to sample any of the snacks. Corn-chip grease and onion dip on my tight white pants would kind of detract from the movie-star image I like to project at a party.

When the number-one hit song came on, some kids got up to dance. Lisa turned up the stereo. She said it was OK to blast it — the neighbors in back were away. My right leg started bouncing to the music without my asking it to.

Richie Kessler walked over to me. He was snarfing down corn chips six at a time, crumbs spewing out the sides of his mouth. Between his mouthful of chips, his shiny braces, and the blaring music, I could hardly understand what he was saying. It was something about the surprise bio quiz.

Now, the last thing I wanted to talk about was the surprise quiz in biology. And the last person I wanted to hang out with was a Definitely Not Sexy guy like Richie Kessler. Besides not being able to talk about anything besides SCHOOL, he has the worse case of acne east of the Mississippi. But I was feeling pretty good in my white jeans and tight T-shirt, and there was my bouncing right leg to consider. So I found myself giving old Richie the benefit of the doubt. I entertained the possibility that beneath his loser exterior beat a heart as secretly sexy as mine.

Before Richie could ask how I'd done on my world history paper or start droning on about the entrance requirements for graduate schools, I said, "C'mon, Rich," and I pulled him onto the patio dance floor. He seemed startled but not unhappy. As for me, I was grateful for the chance to let the rest of my body bounce along with my right leg.

I *love* to dance. Except for when I'm singing along with a record or right after I've been to The Movies, it's the only time I don't feel clumsy and half-baby, half-woman. I'm just all movement and rhythm. I don't worry what people think of me. I just *dance*.

I really started moving and getting into the song.

When it was over, Richie and I danced to the next one. It didn't matter that he danced like a windup robot that was low on batteries. I hardly noticed him. I just listened to the music and felt the beat and moved to it. Half the time my eyes were closed anyway. I could have been dancing by myself.

The next song was a Julie Paris number I really like. Someone turned the stereo up more.

"Won't your parents get mad, Lisa?" asked Billy Munson, who had probably never been to a social event that wasn't sponsored by the Chess Club. "What about the neighbors who *aren't* away?"

Lisa just said, "It's cool," and kept dancing. I could tell that she was high on the music and the party too, and she was probably pretending she was somebody other than Lisa Norris, honors Creep. At that moment I loved Lisa. I just loved her.

I found myself loving everybody at the party. Even Richie Kessler and Billy Munson. Everything felt smooth and easy, just like in The Movies. When I saw Heidi come out onto the patio, I was so happy to see my good friend's freckled face. I just loved her so much. And then the best part of the Julie Paris song came on, where there's a lot of drum beat and less guitar to drown her out. And I found myself grabbing an empty cola bottle for a microphone and launching into my Julie Paris imitation. I clenched the bottle with both hands and sang into it in a tough

101

Julie Paris voice. When the musical interlude started, I got into being Julie even more. I put one hand over my eyes and swung the bottle-microphone around in a circle. Richie Kessler stopped his low-on-batteries-robot dancing and just stared.

Pretty soon everybody on the patio stopped dancing and stood in a kind of circle to watch me. I sang and danced for my audience. And I was I was I *was* Julie Paris. No doubt about it. Totally Julie Paris. At the end of the song, I held my cola-bottle microphone high over my head and took a bow. Just like Julie at the end of her concert movie.

Everybody clapped and yelled "More!" And as I launched into my next number, I caught a glimpse of — I couldn't believe it — Jimmy Peterson in the audience circle. I did my next number, "You Hurt Me, Baby," just for him. I had never been so uninhibited in my life. I moved in ways I'd only moved before in the privacy of my own living room, when Wilma and Zeke were at a garage sale. I was definitely not Diana Pushkin.

By the end of the song, I was pretty wiped out. I announced huskily into my cola bottle, "We're going to take a short break." To the applause of everyone on Lisa Norris's patio, I put down my empty bottle, found a full one, and took a long drink.

"All right, Diana!" said Heidi, suddenly at my side. "You were just like Julie Paris. Just like her!"

"No kidding," I said, catching my breath. "I *am* Julie Paris."

Heidi broke into an appreciative horse's laugh, and then there was a deeper chuckle — Jimmy's. "I finally got to see one of your performances," he said. He looked fine in a green sleeveless T-shirt. His bruised face was almost healed, and his blond hair shone under the patio lights.

Heidi and Jimmy looked at me, waiting for me to say something. I was used to Jimmy doing most of the talking. But now, since I was Julie Paris, words magically formed in my mouth and effortlessly floated out. "Do you two know each other?" I asked. "Heidi, meet Jimmy. Jimmy, meet my good friend Heidi."

"Hi," said Heidi.

"Hi!" said Jimmy. "Always a pleasure to meet a foxy lady."

"Well, I'm on my way to the bathroom," said Heidi. "Nice to meet you, Jimmy." And she left us alone. How I loved Heidi! My friend Heidi, the Fountain.

I wondered what Jimmy was doing at a Creep party, but then I remembered that he had been fired from the Lawson College snack bar and wasn't too popular with the Sexies since word had gotten out about his phony drug deal.

A bunch of other kids came over. "Great show, Diana!" said Lisa.

"Yeah," said Richie Kessler. "What are you on, anyway?"

"Wouldn't you like to know?" I answered. I was sick of people asking me questions like that.

"By the way, Peterson," said Billy Munson, "you've got a nerve showing up here. Lisa said she didn't invite you."

"Billy!" said Lisa. "He's a friend of Diana's."

"I heard there was a party, that's all," said Jimmy, tracing the lines between the patio flagstones with the toe of one of his high-top sneakers. He was about four inches taller than anyone else at the party, making Billy and the other honors Creeps look punier than ever.

"Did you come around to sell some of your phony drugs?" asked Mr. No-Brain Grind, David Cotter.

"Hey, you folks are too smart to fall for that," said Jimmy with a let's-keep-things-light smile.

When no one laughed except me, I said, "Listen, guys, lay off Jimmy. Everybody makes mistakes. Besides, what he did was better than selling real dope!"

"Look who's talking!" Sue Melvin said to me. "The doper of the Junior Honor Society."

"Right!" said Billy. "Probably the only reason you hang around with Jimmy is that he saves some real drugs for you."

"Yeah, what *are* you on tonight, Diana?" asked Richie.

"I'm not high on anything but music," I announced.

"Sure," said Sue, laughing.

"I'm not kidding," I found myself saying. I said it in a way that I meant to be taken seriously. "All this stuff about me and drugs is just a rumor. I've never taken a pill besides Health Drop Chewable Vitamins. I've smoked grass a grand total of twice, and I didn't even like it."

I couldn't believe I had shed one of my major defenses against condemnation to Creepdom, my crazier-than-I-really-am image. "And I don't drink either," I added.

Suddenly, I felt scared. There was a funny feeling in my stomach. Like in this dream I've had a couple of times in which I find myself in math class, and I look down and realize I've forgotten to put on pants. Maybe that's how Jimmy felt when everybody found out about his selling phony drugs. For the first time, I felt as if Jimmy and I had something in common. We both had images we liked to keep up. And they weren't always real.

"Well, I'm sure glad you came tonight, Diana," said Lisa. "You've been the life of the party."

I smiled gratefully at her. Some Creeps really weren't so bad, I decided. I thought things might be OK after all. It was kind of a relief to be honest about the drug thing finally.

Somebody put on a comedy record, and people

105

gradually wandered off to listen to it. Jimmy and I were alone.

"So . . .," he said. He looked into my eyes and touched my hair. I'm not a big authority on beer, since I've only tasted it once and I thought it was mildly disgusting. But when he got close to me, even *I* could tell that his breath reeked of beer.

"So . . .," I said.

"I've known all along that my little Diana wasn't really doing drugs," he said, slurring his words a little. "But you better watch out, giving a rock 'n' roll show like that. You'll turn the boys on."

"Good."

"Come on, don't talk like that, little Diana."

Suddenly, a new plan came to me. I knew how to get past Jimmy's thinking of me as a kid. I knew how to get him to want to fool around with me while still feeling ten years older than me.

"Jimmy," I whispered, still high from being Julie Paris in her concert movie. "Will you teach me? Will you teach me about sex? I've never even kissed anyone, really. What if I went on a date? I wouldn't know what to do, I wouldn't know if a guy was going too far — "

"Do you know what you're asking me?"

"I don't want to go all the way or anything. But I want to go . . . well . . . part way."

Jimmy stared down at me with his brown eyes,

one of which still had a slight bruise around it. "Are you sure?"

"Yes."

"Now?"

"The neighbors in back are away."

He took my hand, and we climbed over a low fence into the dark of the neighboring backyard. There was a sweet smell of newly mown grass. We walked around to the side of the house and stopped under a willow tree that seemed like a canopy over us. Away from the party, we could hear the repetitive chirps of night insects.

Jimmy put his big hands on my shoulders. I felt frightened and stiff. Not at all like Julie Paris.

"Never been kissed," he said. He pressed his beer-tasting lips against mine and thrust his tongue deep into my mouth. So this was how French kissing felt. His tongue darted around in my mouth, and I figured my tongue should dart, too. It did, but it was shy.

Still kissing me, he led me to the ground and lay on top of me, which seemed more serious. I was disappointed that his lips felt hard. Not at all like the soft, melting sensation I had expected from watching The Movies. And the giant pimple on my chin throbbed as *his* chin pushed against it. I started to worry that this whole sex thing was as overrated as smoking dope.

He began to touch and massage my breasts. First through my T-shirt, then under my T-shirt. And then he unhooked my bra to get at them better. I liked that part a lot. I wished I could lie there and have him do that for hours. It felt warm and exciting, the way I had dreamed and imagined sex would be.

Then it occured to me that *I* should be doing something to him. I was already rubbing his neck and back, but I figured that was pretty lightweight stuff compared to what he was doing. Since he didn't have breasts for me to fondle, I thought I should be stroking his crotch. That's what Wendy told me she did to the camp counselor on their second date. But I wasn't ready to touch him there. I told myself I didn't have to. This was just my first lesson.

He shifted his position on top of me so his hard groin hit mine. He started to rub against me, and that felt good. Really good. But part of me couldn't relax because a voice kept chattering in my head, "This is it. . . . You're actually with Jimmy Peterson." And part of me kept being disappointed that his lips were hard and the whole thing was not quite like The Movies. Still another part of me worried that some Creep from the party would wander over and see us there, me lying with my bra off, under Jimmy Peterson, under a willow tree.

The rubbing against me felt wonderful in spite of

my nervousness. Even though Jimmy is much taller than me, we seemed to fit fine. I mean, our crotches met and we could still manage to kiss. I had always wondered how that would work.

Jimmy was breathing fast. I found myself rubbing against *him* and making little noises I had never made before.

All of a sudden, he raised himself off me and unsnapped my white jeans. The snap startled me. He reached down into my underpants.

"No!" I said, and I jumped up. My heart was pounding, and I resnapped my pants and rehooked my bra in record time.

"Hey, Babes, I'm sorry," Jimmy said, standing up too.

"It's OK," I said. "I'm just not ready to lose my virginity or anything."

"Don't worry, you wouldn't have."

Then I got worried about something else. After a minute, I mumbled, "Jimmy, does this mean I'm a prude?" If he thought I was a prude, this would be the last time he would want to "get physical" with me.

"No," he said with a sad laugh. "You're not a prude."

I was relieved to hear his answer. Maybe he would want to do it again sometime. But would *I*? It hadn't been a scene from *The Love Nest*, that was for sure.

I didn't know what to think. I didn't even know how I felt about Jimmy anymore. I was more or less numb.

We started to walk back toward the lights of Lisa Norris's patio. Jimmy kept stumbling over rocks and tree roots. You'd think it would've been easy for us to talk after we'd been pressed against each other for half an hour. But I felt more awkward than I ever had with him.

Finally, I said, "Jimmy, I have to ask you something. . . . Did you . . . did you . . . enjoy it . . . at all?"

"Sure, Babes," he said. He put his hands on my shoulders and kissed the top of my head. I wished his earlier kissing had been as gentle. "How about you? Did you enjoy it?"

"Yes," I said. Well, I had enjoyed part of it.

* 12 *

When Heidi's father drove me home from the party, I reached into the pocket of my white jeans and realized I had left my key at home again. I had been hoping to slip undetected into the house. But now I was forced to knock on the door and face one or both of my parents.

Wilma appeared at the door almost immediately. Apparently, she was still awake, even though it was two hours past her usual ten-o'clock bedtime. Zeke was in bed.

It made me nervous to see Wilma. I felt as if Jimmy's fingerprints were all over my clothing.

Wilma asked me four thousand questions about the party. "How many kids were there? Did you remember to give Mr. and Mrs. Norris my regards?

What did they serve?" As if any of this was important.

Just so she wouldn't suspect that I wasn't her Baby anymore, I tried to answer all her questions. She acted the same as usual. Like any other night, she reminded me to brush my teeth, put my clothes in the hamper, and kiss her good night when she tucked me in.

Then I had trouble sleeping. I was totally confused. All at the same time, I was excited from the kissing and everything, disappointed that it wasn't like The Movies, nervous that people (especially Wilma and Zeke) would find out what I'd done, proud of myself for finally getting some sexual experience, and embarrassed that I had *asked* Jimmy to fool around with me.

The last one was the killer. Had he done it just to be nice? Probably. Or maybe he'd been feeling totally desperate since his supply of college girls had been cut off. *I* must have been pretty desperate to come out and *ask* him like that. He must have thought I was totally pathetic. He had claimed he'd enjoyed it, but he'd probably said that to be polite. On the other hand, he *had* been breathing pretty hard for someone who was just being polite.

Had I blown my one chance to make it with Jimmy Peterson by being nervous and prudish and worrying too much about hard lips?

How I wished we could do it again. But better next time. More like The Movies.

I finally fell asleep and had an awful dream about Jimmy taking me to a movie and then leaving to get popcorn and never coming back. I was the only one in my row, and I could feel the rest of the audience staring at me. If I hadn't slept at all, I would have been better off.

The next day was Saturday, and Heidi came over while Wilma and Zeke hit the garage sales. We sat on my porch steps, across from the Matthewsons' pink house, and talked. I was dying to tell her about Jimmy. But first she made a big deal about being proud of me for admitting that I don't do drugs.

"Yeah, I'm glad I did it, too. I wouldn't want some Creep like Billy Munson shooting smack because he thought someone as cool as I am was doing it," I said with a laugh.

Heidi laughed her horse's laugh. Then she said, "You're not worried about what the Sexies will think when word gets out that your drug story was a fake?"

I had more important things to worry about. "Naah," I said. "Maybe they'll think I'm more interesting for coming up with clever jokes and all when I'm really totally straight. Besides, *I* never said I did drugs. *They're* the ones who started the rumor."

"Well, that's true. You just never denied it before. Speaking of drugs, I'm concerned about Wendy. She told me she's been getting high every single day. I think that's a bit much, don't you?"

"Uh-huh," I said. But I *had* to change the subject to the number-one topic on my mind. "Listen, Heidi, did you notice that I kind of disappeared for a while last night?"

"Yes. I wondered where you were."

"Did you notice that Jimmy disappeared too?"

"I guess so. I thought he went out to get beer or something. Not enough action for him at the party."

"He found some action, all right."

"What do you mean?"

I told Heidi about how I had asked Jimmy to teach me about sex. And I told her what had gone on under the willow tree. Since Heidi and I are such good friends and since her bugged-out eyes told me she was very much interested, I gave her plenty of details, even about how I didn't want to touch Jimmy's private parts. I didn't feel like telling her that his lips were hard and that his chin had hit my pimple and that I was kind of nervous the whole time and that it wasn't exactly a scene from *The Love Nest*.

By the time I finished my story, I was feeling

114

pretty pumped up for having made out with a guy I'd had a crush on for months and who looked like he was nineteen and who I considered Definitely Sexy even if Heidi didn't. Up until that half hour with Jimmy the night before, the only times I had felt at all sexy were when I was pretending to be someone else.

Heidi gave me a weird look.

"What's the matter?" I asked. "Do I look different or something now that I'm a woman?"

"Jeez, Diana," she said. "I can't believe you *asked* him to fool around with you. And you're not even going out with him or anything and you let him play with your boobs."

"Maybe I'm not going out with him, but we're good friends."

"Sounds like you're more than friends."

I giggled wickedly. Heidi looked at me and wrinkled her freckled nose.

"What's that for?" I asked.

"*I'm* going to wait until I'm in love with a guy and he's in love with me before I do more than kiss someone."

"Yes, you've told me. And I always tell *you* I don't want to wait that long. The way things are going, with all the Creeps in our classes, I probably won't fall in love until college. You're not about to fall in love with Richie Kessler, are you? Or how about

David Cotter, if he stops studying long enough to notice there are two sexes?"

I waited for Heidi to break into her horse's laugh, but she just sat there, looking disapproving. I said, "I'm sure I didn't do anything the Sexies haven't been doing since junior high. I'm tired of being Definitely Not Sexy."

"I can't get over you," she said. "You came on to him. He had beer on his breath. You sound like a . . . a . . . whore!"

"Give me a break, Heidi," I said.

"Listen, Diana, let me give you some advice. Just watch yourself. You don't want to end up with AIDS. And you don't want to get a rep."

I reminded her that I hadn't gone all the way or anything. And I'd *had* to ask Jimmy, or he would have gone on treating me like a baby.

I gave her some great arguments. I could have convinced the Pope, and maybe even Wilma. But by the time Heidi left, I was a wreck. If my good friend thought I was a whore, what would non-friends say?

I mean, what if Jimmy spread the story all over school? I didn't *think* he would. In spite of what everybody said about Jimmy, I felt I could trust him.

But what if I couldn't? After all, hadn't he told *me* all kinds of details about his dates with his college girlfriends? What would stop him from telling half of Beechurst High about our — my God — practically having sexual intercourse under the willow tree? By the time the story got around, it would be that we *did* have intercourse.

And I had asked him to! He would say I'd seduced him. I could just hear him: "I had a couple beers. And this chick Diana starts coming on to me. . . ." He would even have witnesses. All the honors Creeps at the party had seen me doing my wildest Julie Paris number, wearing my tightest T-shirt. Maybe they had even seen us take off for the neighbor's yard.

My reputation was about to make another turnaround. I could imagine conversations in the halls: "Did you hear about Diana Pushkin? Remember we thought she was a straight, boring, smart, goody-goody? Then we heard otherwise — she's a druggy. OK, then it's no drugs, but she's on the, shall we say, *promiscuous* side. Let's face it, the kid is a whore!"

In just one night, I had stepped over the line from goody-goody baby to slut. I'll tell you what burned me up more than anything — if I was going to be branded as a whore, I should at least have had a better time!

13

After Heidi left, I spent the rest of the day being depressed about becoming a loose woman. Heidi was right. I'd better watch myself, or I'd be a nymphomaniac by tenth grade.

I was in a bad mood as it was. And then Wilma came up to me, waving the white jeans I'd worn the night before. "Honestly, Baby," she said, "you shouldn't sit on the grass when you wear white pants." Then she gave me her lecture 11A — "When you grow up and you're responsible for your own laundry, you'll take better care of your clothes."

I felt like telling her I had done more than *sit* on the grass the night before.

I tried to get my mind off things by reading this book about the psychoanalyst Sigmund Freud. It

118

was complicated reading, but I really liked it. It's all about what makes people tick. And there was an especially neat section about what Freud said different dreams mean. It seemed that a lot of dreams have to do with sex, which didn't surprise me at all. Anyway, I was in the living room, trying to read my book, when I heard Wilma talking on the phone, as usual.

"Guess what Diana's reading on her own?" she said. "A book on Freud! A lot of people twice her age couldn't plow through it!"

It really made me angry to hear her telling people what I was doing. It was none of their business. I swear, she was still treating me like one of her nursery-school kids. I used to put up with this treatment in order to keep my private life and thoughts to myself. But now I was sick of it.

Wilma was still showing off about me the same way she must have when I was a baby — "Diana turned over by herself today!" "Diana said 'Bye-bye' today!" "Diana peed in the potty today!" And now it was "Diana's reading Freud today!"

I was in such a foul mood that I felt like yanking the receiver out of her hand and yelling into it, "Diana got felt up last night!"

I controlled myself and concentrated on a chapter on dreams. It said that when you dream about a snake or a stick, it's really about a penis. Suddenly, my reading was interrupted. Wilma was off the phone and had nothing better to do than sink down next to me on the yellow couch with blue flowers and bother me. "What vegetable would you like with meat loaf tonight, Baby?" she asked.

"I'm trying to read!" I found myself shouting. "And Jesus Christ, I'm not a baby!" I threw the book about Freud clear across the living room. It almost knocked over one of the six thousand bud vases Wilma and Zeke have bought at garage sales. About two thousand are in the living room, cluttering shelves and cabinets, and the other four thousand are in the basement with other supposedly useful garage-sale treasures.

"Will you watch your language?" said Wilma. "You kids are so disrespectful" (Wilma's lecture 18A).

"I'll talk how I goddamned well please!" I said, determined that she would never think of me as Baby again. I was furious enough to drop my Baby image and risk having my parents suspect that I have my own life with certain thoughts and actions they might disapprove of.

Wilma and I were noisy enough for Zeke to hear us from the den, where he was catching up on his life-insurance paperwork. He lumbered in to ask, "What seems to be the problem?"

"Diana doesn't want us to call her Baby," explained Wilma in an isn't-she-being-ridiculous? tone of voice.

Zeke chuckled, which made me even angrier. "I know you're growing up," he said. "But we'll always think of you as our baby. Someday — "

" — you'll understand," I said at the same time he did. "That's your lecture sixteen-B."

"You don't have to be fresh," said Zeke, his forehead reddening.

"Just leave me alone," I barked, getting up.

"What about the vegetable tonight, Baby — I mean, Diana?" Wilma asked in a let's-get-back-to-what's-really-important tone of voice.

As clearly as possible I enunciated, *"I don't give a shit."* I stomped upstairs to my room, leaving them with their arms crossed over their blubbery stomachs and bewildered expressions on their faces.

Alone in my room, I wondered if I had gone too far, if I would regret closing the door to being Baby. Maybe it would be like Wilma's lecture 17A, about garage-sale snack tables and makeup — "You can never tell when you might need it."

I felt scared and exposed, the way I had the night before, after I announced that I'm not into drugs after all. Part of me wanted to cry over the fact that I couldn't run to Mommy and Daddy like in the good old days, bury my face in their comforting, comfortable shoulders, and tell them everything that was wrong. My eyes burned with tears I wouldn't let out.

The next day, Sunday, I was in an even more terrible mood, if that's possible. I decided there was only one thing that would help — The Movies. I had to find a way to make being sad and confused feel dramatic instead of just a drag.

I told Wilma, who was a bit cold to me after our scene the day before, that I was headed for a matinee. Instead of her usual "Have fun, Baby" and warm smile, she said, "Here's two dollars. Bring home a half gallon of ninety-nine-percent-fat-free milk. *Ninety-nine-percent fat-free.* And bring me the change."

The Beechurst Cinema was showing *Him and Her* starring Jacqueline Chase and Richard Delton, both of whom have absolutely gorgeous turquoise eyes. I set off alone, of course, so no one could step on my dramatic mood. I wore sneakers in order to bop along afterward and feel graceful. And I put on sunglasses to feel glamorous and to keep the lights from shocking me when they suddenly flashed on at the end.

On the way in, I noticed a new worker emptying ash trays in the lobby. Maybe my tattooed propositioner had been fired. I hoped so.

As soon as I sank into the plush velvet movie seat, I relaxed. I felt as if everything would be OK, no matter what had happened or not happened at Lisa Norris's party, and no matter what Wilma or Zeke or anyone in the town of Beechurst thought of me. There were *four* coming attractions, so I felt really lucky. I *love* coming attractions. You get to see all the good parts without the boring ones.

The movie was a comic love story about an Army major and a woman peace activist. There were some funny lines, and the romantic scenes were sexy and beautiful. By the end, I was Jacqueline Chase, or at least the peace activist she played.

Before the lights could get me, I whipped on my sunglasses and left the theater for a walk. Or rather, in the movie-star state of mind I was in, a float. Main Street was crowded on this hot June afternoon. People were armed with ice cream cones, radios, and giant pretzels. I sailed through the crowd, feeling I had the power to change Don't Walk signs to Walk signs just by placing my foot on the curb. A surprising number of guys resembled my costar, Richard Delton. I reminded myself that Diana Pushkin, like Jacqueline Chase, had been kissed in the night and had laid down with a man.

I was very much aware that underneath my sunglasses lurked a pair of turquoise eyes, twice as large as my usual hazel ones. And though I had a nagging feeling that something *had* been bothering me, I felt my life was being filmed for The Movies. Every step I took, every turn of my head to glance into a store window, was being caught on film.

I drifted into the duck-pond park, where toddlers were squealing over greedy ducks and parents were snapping photos of the toddlers. Bare-chested boys were throwing Frisbees and swearing. It was all my private movie set.

My body slid onto a bench as effortlessly as maple syrup pouring onto French toast. I took out a cigarette. Wendy, who smokes about a pack a month (at parties and when her parents go away for the weekend), had given it to me, and I had been saving it for the right occasion. Sitting on a bench at the duck-pond park after seeing *Him and Her* seemed like the right moment. I wanted to enhance my movie-star image, even though smoking is awful for you and the one time I had tried it I'd gotten so dizzy I'd almost passed out, right in my own bathroom.

The cigarette was a little bent from hanging around in my pocketbook for a month, but I tried to ignore that. I placed it between my sensuous Jacqueline Chase lips and struck a match. It went out. I struck another match and tried to shield the flame from a suddenly strong breeze, but it blew out before it got near the cigarette. After the third match, the filter was getting damp.

This whole scene was starting to threaten my mood, because Jacqueline Chase not being able to light a cigarette did not make sense in the movie that was playing in my head. When I had used up all the matches, I got an idea — I could just sit there holding and dragging on an unlit cigarette! It was certainly healthier that way — it posed no risks to my heart or lungs — and there was no danger of coughing or getting dizzy.

After I decided that the park scene was finished being filmed (and the cigarette filter was hopelessly damp), I tossed the cigarette into a trash barrel and set off for Central Supermarket to pick up Wilma's stupid milk. I waltzed through the automatic door, savoring the power of controlling things with a stamp of my foot. Floating down the aisles to the dairy department, I bopped along with the understated rhythm of the piped-in supermarket music. I located a half gallon of 99-percent-fat-free milk, making sure to smile for the camera that was recording the scene on film, and sailed over to the express line.

The checker was not the "How ya doin' today? Hot enough for ya?" type. She was cold and distant, in a world of her own, with vegetable prices — and secret dreams, perhaps — dancing in her head. On other days her aloofness might have caused me to get nervous (Am I such a wimp that no one even notices me?), but not today.

With ease, grace, and the promise of drama, I

put the change in my wallet and picked up the brown paper bag. And then my whole world collapsed. Now, that may sound overdramatic, but the person who had waltzed into Central Supermarket with the Jacqueline Chase eyes and smile never got a chance to float back out the automatic door. She was assassinated.

You see, there's this mirror that takes up an entire wall, right beyond the checkout counter. I had forgotten all about it, and I just wasn't prepared for it. There I was, feeling like a movie star, but when I glanced at my reflection, I saw a short, slightly overweight kid wearing sunglasses that were too big for her, a denim jacket that was buttoned wrong, and baggy jeans with popcorn grease on the thighs. To top things off, she had a bulging pimple on her chin and pieces of cigarette filter in her teeth. She started to whimper.

I cried most of the way home. The only reason I stopped was that somewhere in the vicinity of This-Is-a-Deli, I changed from depressed to furious. The object of my wrath was moviemakers. They have *some nerve*, sucking you into their technicolor world and then sending you out into the crummy, real world.

They trap you in this totally dark theater (except for a couple of red Exit signs), and the seats are so comfortable that you can't feel your rear end. You can't help being riveted to the bigger-than-life screen and starting to think that everyone is either gorgeous or has such a great accent that he or she might as well be gorgeous. And the background music comes on at all the right times. The record never skips.

And everyone is *sooooo* sexy. No one has acne. When a man and a woman look at each other, they have absolute communication. They melt into each other's arms. You can just tell that no one has hard lips.

And where do they get all these actors with turquoise eyes? I mean, I know about three people with really blue eyes. Most people have perfectly ordinary brown or hazel eyes, like me. But in The Movies, just about everybody's got breathtaking turquoise eyes. It's not fair at all.

I fumed all the way home about how The Movies trick you into thinking things are five thousand times better than they really are.

I stomped up my driveway, past the depressing frog-sitting-on-a-mushroom sculptures, up the porch steps, and into the house. I handed Wilma the 99-percent-fat-free milk and her change. Instead of saying thank you in her usual sweet way, she started carrying on about how the date on the carton was that day's date, and didn't I know anything about expiration dates, and how did I expect the milk to stay fresh, and couldn't she trust me with anything?

That last part about trusting me really bugged me, since I was feeling weird about what had gone on at Lisa Norris's and all. Maybe my reputation as a whore had already spread from Jimmy and the other kids at the party to their mothers and all the way to Wilma.

I was feeling so mad about the moviemakers and so sad that I couldn't confide in Wilma the way I used to — I mean, I can't exactly cry on her shoulder and complain that making out with Jimmy Peterson wasn't as good as it looks in The Movies, or about anything that's been going on in my head lately — that I said, "No, I guess you can't trust me with anything. I'm just a goddamned juvenile delinquent." And I ran up to my room and slammed the door and wouldn't come down for dinner.

14

The next day was the third-to-last day of school before summer vacation. The last Monday of the school year! I should have been in a terrific mood, but I felt horrible after the horribleness of the weekend.

At breakfast, Wilma and Zeke and I said about two words to each other.

And in homeroom, Paula Proomer asked me, "No jokes this morning?"

"Not today," I mumbled, wishing she would quit pretending to like me.

After homeroom, I avoided Jimmy in the hall. I knew I would have to face him eventually, but I wanted to put it off for as long as possible.

I hardly heard a word my teachers said all morning. Come to think of it, I probably didn't miss much.

At lunch, Wendy and I sat alone at a table. I must have looked as rotten as I felt because she said, "What's the matter? The oven-baked chicken is pretty disgusting, but it's nothing to go into a depression about."

I told her I had far worse problems than the school lunch. I said I was angry at the world, and especially moviemakers.

"Hey, you're just finding out life is not The Movies?" Wendy said. "If movies were like real life, nobody would pay to see them because they'd be too boring. I mean, they're not going to show every time somebody does their laundry or goes to the bathroom to take a leak."

I had to laugh at Wendy's way of explaining things. "But do they have to make sex seem so smooth and easy?" I asked. I whispered to her about Jimmy and me at Lisa's party, including the disappointing parts that I hadn't even told Heidi.

"You devil," she said with a wink. "Well, hey, you were nervous with Jimmy. You have such a crush on him. No wonder you felt awkward."

"I guess so."

"Someday you'll feel more like you're kissing on the silver screen. You just have to wait for the right chemistry."

"Don't depress me even more. I'm taking *chemistry* next year with Mr. ("Ass") Aston. '*Stew*dents, keep it down, *stew*dents!'"

"Very funny, Diana. Well, you must be feeling better if you're making jokes, as usual."

"Yeah, I feel a little better. But Wen, do you think I went too far? I mean, was it like really forward of me to ask Jimmy to . . . you know?"

"Oh, keep your shirt on, Diana."

"Maybe that's what I should have done Friday night."

Wendy broke into her chicken-cackle laugh. Then she said, "Seriously, life is short. You gotta do what you feel like. Besides, you didn't even go all the way, like I have."

"Yes, you've told me all about it at least twelve times. In great detail."

"Well, hey, an extraordinary story bears repeating."

Suddenly, I started to feel nervous again. "Wendy, what if Jimmy starts to repeat the story about him and me? I don't want what we did to get all over school. I mean, I've never been on a date with Jimmy, except to ride around my neighborhood in a borrowed car (maybe it was even stolen!), and you can't really call that a date, and now I let him — I practically *asked* him to — reach into my underpants!"

"Calm down, Diana! I haven't heard a *word* of gossip about you."

"Good. I don't want to get a reputation as a slut."

"Read my lips! YOU ARE NOT — I REPEAT — YOU ARE NOT A SLUT."

"Ssh!" I said. Then I realized that no one could possibly have heard what she had said. Between plates clattering and hundreds of conversations, the cafeteria was ten times louder than Ms. "Enthusiasm" Bladadorph's piano attack at the Junior Honor Society assembly. It was even louder than the music at Wendy's dope party.

"You are not a slut," Wendy repeated more softly. "You went to a party and fooled around with a friend. Period."

Talking with good old Wendy really cheered me up. She seemed to think anything I did was OK, and I started to feel that my problems weren't the end of the world.

After a while, Roseanne Capullo sat down with us. She mostly talked to Wendy, not to me. I was afraid it was because she had heard about my exploits at Lisa's party and didn't approve of them. I was sure I hadn't done anything Roseanne herself hadn't done. But she has a steady boyfriend, so it's different. Besides, Roseanne is one of the Sexies, and I'm supposed to be one of the smart Definitely Nots, so I figured she thought I had a lot of nerve acting like that. I was a Creep *and* a whore — a nauseating combination.

I glanced over at Paula Proomer, two tables over. *She* certainly has a rep, as Heidi calls it, but everybody accepts that that's the way she's supposed to be. Paula is so gorgeous, it would be almost selfish of her not to share herself.

Suddenly, I realized that Roseanne was talking to Wendy about brands of birth-control pills and which ones made her get the fewest pimples. I guess I started staring at her.

"Sorry, Diana," she said. "You wouldn't know about things like this."

I couldn't help it — I burst out laughing. And Wendy started cackling like a chicken again. Apparently, Wendy was right. Roseanne hadn't heard the word that I'm a whore after all. Probably everybody still thinks of me as a boring honors Creep who, as it turns out, doesn't even do drugs. I don't know which of my potential images is worst — slut or Creep. Frankly, I'm not wild about the choices.

Roseanne left to sit at Paula Proomer's table, and soon Heidi joined us. I was glad to see that Heidi wasn't through with me just because she thought I was on my way to becoming a nymphomaniac. Wendy, Heidi, and I talked about our plans for the summer. They're pretty dismal. None of us has a job, and we're too old for camp. We all agreed that vacation will be heavenly anyway, just to not be in school.

"Did Wendy tell you her news?" Heidi asked me.

"What news?" I said.

"She's cutting down on dope," said Heidi.

"Good idea, Wen," I said. I felt bad that I had been so caught up with my own problems that I had forgotten about Wendy's.

"Yeah, things were getting a little out of hand," said Wendy. "The old brain was getting fuzzy, you know? Fred and I are both cutting way down."

I was thinking how glad I was that in spite of my troubles, my award-winning, Honor Society brain was still sharp when Wendy and Heidi suddenly got quiet and looked down at their half-eaten lunches. I turned around, and there was Jimmy. He should have been in health class, but I guess he was skipping it.

"Excuse me, can I talk to you, Diana?" he asked. I had never seen him act so unsure of himself. Usually, he would have said something like, "Ladies! Mind if a handsome guy like me joins you?"

I was super-embarrassed to see him. At the same time, I was as excited as ever to be near him.

"Well, hey, I was just leaving," said Wendy, getting up.

"That's OK, you don't — " I started to say.

"I gotta go, too," said Heidi.

And they were gone, leaving me alone with Jimmy and a piece of oven-baked chicken. I was too embarrassed to look at him.

"You ran off after homeroom," he said as he sat down across from me.

"I had to get something from my locker."

Jimmy's dark eyes stared at me. He wasn't convinced. "Is it because of . . . you know . . . the other night?"

The pounding of my heart was as loud as the lunch trays being dumped into the dirty-plates window. I tried to sound casual. "The other night? Oh, that."

"I was kind of out of it, I guess," said Jimmy. "I had a bunch of beers with this guy I'm going in on a business deal with, and — "

My concern about Jimmy made me forget my embarrassment. "Business deal?" I said. "Jimmy, don't get yourself in trouble again!"

"No, no trouble this time. But listen, uh . . . are you sorry about, uh . . . what happened? I mean, I'm . . . well . . . worried that I took advantage of you."

I thought how ironic it was that Jimmy and I were both feeling guilty about our willow-tree rendezvous. And he was actually concerned about me. I always knew he was a much better person than the rest of Beechurst High gave him credit for.

I found myself making light of my confused feelings in order to protect *his* feelings. "Don't worry, Jimmy," I said. "I'm not sorry at all. Now I'll know what to do when My Man walks into my life! Besides, you didn't take advantage of me — I was the one who asked you. Remember?"

Jimmy seemed to think about this for a while. Then he said, "Yeah, but you're only a kid. I should have said no, but I was half in the bag."

"I'm *not* a kid. Tell me, did you feel like you were with a kid?"

I couldn't believe I'd had the nerve to ask him that. To my surprise, he answered, "Nooooo." And he raised an eyebrow in his sexy way. "You felt like a WOMAN to me."

He seemed to mean it about my feeling like a woman. Maybe he really *had* enjoyed it. The look in his eyes kind of turned me on, the way I had felt during the good parts under the willow tree. Then I remembered my reputation. . . .

"Jimmy, um . . . you won't tell anyone about what happened? Or about my asking you or anything, will you?"

"No, I promise. But promise *me* something." He looked around and then lowered his voice. "Don't tell anyone I've been worrying about taking advantage of you. People will think I've gone soft or something. Might hurt my reputation as a lady-killer."

"I promise."

"I've been wanting to say . . . uh . . . something else. . . . Thanks for sticking by me through all the crap that came down about the college thing. . . . I mean, sometimes I feel like you're the only person in this school who still talks to me."

"You'll always be pretty terrific by me."

Jimmy grinned. "Listen, I'll never forget you for standing up for me at that party. I want to thank you, now that I'm sober."

"You're very welcome," I slurred, as if *I* were suddenly totally drunk.

Jimmy cracked up. When he stopped laughing, he looked really serious, and I was afraid to hear what he would say. Finally, he asked, "Can we still be friends? It's funny, but I really count on talking to you every day."

"Sure," I said, and I was surprised to feel relieved that he wanted to be my friend, not my lover. I didn't know why, but that was what I wanted now, too.

I still felt he was the most exciting person I'd ever known. But suddenly I decided that even though he could pass for nineteen and I could be mistaken for ten and a half, in a lot of ways *I* was more grown up than he was.

When the bell rang, I gathered up my books for Honors English and watched my hero, Jimmy, bounce off to Regular Algebra. I thought about how Jimmy didn't have parents around to talk to. But he had me. I felt kind of proud that, now that I thought of it, I *had* stood by him, as he'd said. Maybe Heidi was right about my being a good person, even if I wasn't exactly movie-star material.

The annoying thing was that no matter what I did, Jimmy and everyone else thought of me as a little kid. When would I meet someone WHO DIDN'T TREAT ME LIKE A BABY?

I did hope Jimmy and I could stay friends, as odd a pair as we were. Mr. Sexy Man about Town and Miss Goody Two Shoes. Peterson and Pushkin. At least we would always be in the same homeroom.

15

I'm glad school is over for the summer now, but I
don't have anything special planned. My only def-
inite employment opportunity is feeding the Matthewsons' cat for two weeks in August while the
Matthewsons go to Canada.

When it comes to entertainment, I'm not like the
Sexies, who all seem to have been born having a
friend with a driver's license. I'm pretty much stuck
going places within walking distance or getting my
parents to drive me. As for the idea of Wilma and
Zeke taking me along to the beach — well, I'd rather
eat rat poison.

Speaking of old Zilma and Weke, things aren't
too bad between us. We've cooled off since I blew
up at Wilma for calling me Baby and annoying me

about what vegetable I wanted with meat loaf. After the three of us stopped being angry with each other, we were kind of awkward. I had made a big deal about being Diana the grown-up and not Diana the Baby, and then I didn't know how to talk to them. They didn't seem to know what to say, either.

Last Saturday morning, as usual, they headed out for Garage-Sale Land. I used their absence to play my new Julie Paris record full blast on the living-room stereo while I practiced singing along into a bud-vase "microphone." An hour and a half later, when Wilma and Zeke pulled into the driveway, I turned off the stereo, put the bud vase back in the china closet (along with about five hundred other bud vases), and sat down with a book I'm reading about the artist Vincent van Gogh.

"Oh, hi," I said when Wilma and Zeke came in.

They both looked extremely pleased with themselves. Wilma grinned, and Zeke's eyes sparkled behind his clear-framed eyeglasses. "We have a surprise!" announced Zeke.

Oh no, I thought. Another stuffed animal.

Zeke waddled out into the hall and came back struggling with a huge carton.

Damn! I thought. A stuffed gorilla.

"Look inside, Diana!" said Wilma, as excited as one of her nursery-school kids bringing home a valentine she'd made.

140

I peeked in the carton and — I couldn't believe it — there was a stereo turntable and speakers inside.

"For your room!" said Wilma. "They said it's practically brand-new!"

I was shocked. "Wow!" was all I could say.

"You see," said Wilma, "we *do* realize our Baby is growing up. We know you have your own taste in music and your own ideas about things."

"You do?" I said. It was pretty hard for me to believe. Maybe they did realize I had my own opinions, but I was sure they weren't happy about it. I was sure they would much rather I stayed their Baby.

"And look, we got you headphones, so you can play your music as loud as you want!" said Zeke.

"You guys!" I said. "This is fantastic!"

"We knew you'd want your own stereo because we know you like privacy now," said Wilma with a sigh. "Also . . . well . . . I guess it's not too exciting for you to hang around with us."

"Oh, Wilma, I like to hang out with you guys . . . sometimes. Thanks a million — a trillion — for the stereo. You are great!" I grabbed them both into a giant, three-way hug. We hadn't had one of those in ages. And I have to admit that even though I *am* kind of old to get a kick out of a three-way hug, and even though it was a little like being crushed between two mountains, the hug felt pretty good.

After a while, I said, "You know how you mentioned that I'm growing up and I have my own ideas and all? Well . . . do you guys . . . still . . . like me anyway?"

"Are you kidding?" bellowed Zeke. "Of course!"

"We love you!" said Wilma.

And they hugged me so hard that I had to tell them to take it easy.

Unfortunately, the garage-sale stereo was not in exactly perfect condition. To put it bluntly, it didn't work. Zeke spent all that Saturday afternoon, when he could have been watching a baseball game on TV, fiddling with the stereo. He kept swearing and then apologizing to me for his language, and going down to the basement to find different tools.

In the end the thing had to spend a week at the repair shop, and the bill was twice what they'd paid for it in the first place. But it's working pretty well now. And somehow their buying me that old stereo did a lot to patch things up between us in a new and better way.

Just the same, I'm not thrilled about being home with Wilma and Zeke all summer and hearing how sloppy and disrespectful, etc., etc., we kids are. Some things, like Wilma's and Zeke's lectures, never change.

One day during the second week of vacation, Wendy invited me over. Her cousin Jack from Minnesota had arrived. Both of Jack's parents work full-time, and his older brothers have jobs in summer camps. So instead of rattling around an empty house, he's staying with Wendy's family for the summer. Did I want to come over and do nothing with her and Jack? Wendy called to ask.

"Sure," I said. But I made up my mind to tell them I didn't want to smoke dope. It makes me feel too crazy, and besides, Wendy is supposed to be reducing her dope consumption.

It was a really hot day. I put on sunglasses, a purple T-shirt, and navy-blue, shiny shorts (which I, not Wilma, had actually picked out) and walked over to Wendy's. I made the walk more interesting by pretending I was in a movie being filmed in an African desert. It made sweating profusely feel dramatic instead of just plain gross.

As soon as I got to Wendy's, I noticed that her cousin Jack was cute. He had brown curly hair and a great twinkle in his eyes. He wasn't manly-looking like Jimmy. But he was, as Heidi would say, sensitive-looking. He and Wendy were sitting under a maple tree in the backyard, drinking lemonade.

Wendy poured me a glass, and the three of us

started talking. I could tell Jack felt shy. I did too. I wished I had Wendy's smooth blond hair and slim figure.

We complained about how hot it was, but we agreed that it was better to be hot than cold. Then we went on to which beach had the biggest waves and what color hair was most becoming for Wendy's mother. She changes her hair color almost as often as she goes away for weekends. Thinking about it made me kind of grateful for Wilma's never-changing, mousy-brown hair.

Wendy insisted that "Mother Dear" looked best as a redhead. I favored black.

"How about a rainbow effect?" asked Jack.

I burst out laughing at the idea of Wendy's mother with a big multicolored head of hair, like some far-out rock singer. I could tell Jack was pleased that he had made me laugh. His brown eyes twinkled even more, and he seemed to relax. So did I. I even took off my sunglasses.

We started talking about movies, and it seemed as if Jack has seen just about everything.

"When I like a movie, I might see it three or four times," he said. "I end up memorizing lines. I guess I really get into movies."

"Me too," I said. Then I found myself saying, "A lot of times after a movie, I feel like I'm one of the characters." That's not the kind of thing I usually confide to someone I hardly know. But Jack was easy to talk to. Besides, I was as tired of trying to act cooler than I am in front of kids my age as I was of acting more naive than I am in front of Wilma and Zeke. Both kinds of pretending could be a real strain.

"I know what you mean about feeling like you're in the movies," said Jack. "Yeah!"

Wendy just sat there smiling during most of our conversation. She knows only too well what a movie maniac I am. Suddenly, she stood up and said she had to make a phone call. Behind Jack's back, she winked at me. I felt like yelling at her and hugging her at the same time.

When Wendy left, Jack and I both got shy again. We stared down at the ground and rotated our glasses of lemonade, jiggling the ice.

Finally, Jack said quietly, "Wendy told me you're really smart in school."

"Well . . . I don't know . . ." I said lamely. There go my chances with this guy, I thought.

"Not a bad combination — smart *and* cute," he said with a shy, twinkly smile.

I smiled back at him. I was thinking, He actually likes me!

We were both quiet again. Then Jack said, "Well, we *have* to go to a movie together. I mean, after the conversation we just had, it would be totally crazy not to. Don't you think?"

I laughed. "I guess you're right."

By the time Wendy returned from her supposed phone call, Jack and I had agreed to go see a movie starring the English singer-actress Nina Castle. The next night.

While I walked home, I thought how great it was that I had met a guy who was smart and cute, which is what he'd said about me. He actually *appreciated* my being smart, instead of thinking intelligence was an unfortunate trait that made me a Creep. Not only was he smart, but he had a good sense of humor. And a good sense of humor is something you don't find every day.

I thought how lucky it was that Jack was from far away in Minnesota instead of Beechurst. I mean, if he went to my high school, he might be one of the Sexies because he was cute, and he wouldn't have anything to do with me. But he was also smart, so maybe he'd be one of the Junior Honors Creeps. And in that case, he wouldn't have anything to do with me because Creeps don't want much to do with Creeps either.

It was my first real date, and Wilma and Zeke were nervous. That made three of us.

"What time do you think you'll be home?" Zeke asked me during dinner. "Around nine?"

"Nine!" I said. "The movie doesn't *start* until eight-oh-five!"

"It's dark by nine," Zeke said, trying to sound casual, it seemed.

"I won't be alone," I said. I gathered from the red color of Zeke's forehead that this did not make him any less nervous. He didn't say anything more about my plans for the evening. But he had only one helping of tuna-noodle casserole.

Later, while Wilma and I were doing the dishes, she said, "Your father wants me to tell you something." Then she didn't say what it was. She just kept washing the dishes and handing them to me to load into the dishwasher. I have given up arguing against Zeke's rule that the dishes need to be pre-washed before going into the dishwasher. But sometimes I wonder if my family could be arrested for wasting energy.

"What does Zeke want you to tell me?" I asked. "Why doesn't he tell me whatever it is himself?"

"You know how he is," said Wilma. She stared at a blue and white trivet on the wall instead of at me.

"Oh, it's about sex!" I said cheerily.

"Diana! Well, yes, if you have to put it so crassly. It's just that your father wants to make sure you know that he does not approve of, um . . . you know . . . petting."

"What? Why not?" I asked, trying not to laugh.

"Well, it's just not healthy for young people."

I couldn't help teasing Wilma. "You mean, it's healthier for older people?" I asked.

147

"No, I don't mean that. . . . I . . . ."

"Tell Zeke I'll give his concerns serious consideration," I said, putting Wilma out of her misery.

Wilma seemed to breathe for the first time in minutes. "I'm sure he'll be relieved," she said.

Naturally, it took me ages to decide what to wear. Should I chance makeup again? Should I try to look sexy or just be comfortable? I finally decided on a jeans and blouse outfit that I thought was flattering but not particularly sexy. Instead of trying to look like someone I wasn't, I actually wanted Jack to get to know me. I didn't put on makeup or hide behind sunglasses. I even combed my bangs to the side so he could see my eyes. At the same time, I was absolutely terrified that he might be turned off by what he saw.

From the guest-room window I watched for Jack. I was kind of afraid he wouldn't show up. Then I spotted him coming up the porch steps, his curly hair bouncing as he walked. Now I was really afraid. He was even cuter than I had remembered. How could *I* have such a great-looking date?

I managed to yell, "Bye, guys, see you later," and bound out the door before I had to let Jack in and introduce him to Wilma and Zeke and stand around awkwardly for ten minutes.

"Hi," Jack said. I was surprised and delighted to see from his twinkling eyes that he really liked me, and that *he* didn't think of me as a little kid. I hoped I would have the chance to go against Zeke's advice as soon as possible.

We walked down the driveway, past the frog-sitting-on-a-mushroom sculptures and onto the street, past the Matthewsons' pink house. The crickets were making a racket.

After "How's Wendy doing?" and "Pretty good — she hasn't smoked a joint in four days," we both seemed to have trouble thinking of something to say. I barely knew Jack, so it was hard to make conversation about the kind of stuff you bring up if you already know someone. For instance, I couldn't say, "Does your dog still have worms?" or "What's your friend Chuck doing this summer?" or "Isn't the study-hall monitor a drag?" Also, Jack wasn't like Jimmy, rapping on about himself all the time.

I tried to survive the walk to the Beechurst Cinema by pretending that I was the peace activist played by Jacqueline Chase in *Him and Her*, and that I had something so heavy on my mind that I didn't want to make small talk.

In the ticket line, I spotted Paula Proomer. We said hi to each other. I noticed her giving Jack the once-over. I knew I would never have the nerve to look at a guy like that, and I felt babyish and inferior. Even though I had just given myself a lecture at home on trying to look like myself for a change, I couldn't help comparing my comfortable jeans and sneakers unfavorably with Paula's tight black pants and high-heeled sandals.

I had peed at home right before I left. But I was so nervous that I had to again. I was as bad as Heidi the Fountain.

I told Jack I would meet him in the lobby.

When I came out of the ladies' room, still recovering from having seen myself in The Mirror (my enemy) and deciding that I had chosen an absolutely atrocious outfit, that my face (which I hadn't chosen) wasn't much better, and that there was no way anyone could possibly be attracted to me, I saw Jack talking with Paula. I figured that he had taken one look at her and concluded that Beechurst had better things to offer than yours truly. Well, I wasn't going to fight against that kind of competition. I decided the best course of action was to bow out gracefully and sneak out of the theater.

But Jack seemed to be looking for me. "Diana!" he called.

As I slunk over to him, he said, "I just met the girl who sits in front of you in homeroom. How's that for a coincidence?"

"Hi, Paula," I said, my voice a pathetic peep.

"Hello," she said huskily. "How's your summer been so far?"

"Not bad. Yours?"

"Just OK. Listen, nice to run into you. There's my date. I'll see you later."

Even though it turned out that Paula was waiting for someone else (a really handsome guy), I figured Jack must be pretty depressed to have seen the Queen of the Sexies and now be stuck with four-foot-eleven, plain me.

On the way to our seats, I said, "Paula's gorgeous, isnt she?" just so he would know that *I* knew I wasn't in the same league.

"She's all right," he said. "Not my type, though."

"What do you mean?"

"Oh, I don't know. She's a little too . . . too much. You know, heavy on the makeup and all."

"Oh."

"She sure likes *you,* though."

"What do you mean?"

"Oh, she went on and on about you. 'You're with Diana Pushkin?' she said. 'She's a great kid. She's brilliant but not stuck up. And you should hear the comments she makes in homeroom. She could be on TV or something!' "

"Paula just walked up to you and started talking about *me?*"

"Yeah. I guess she figured she'd be friendly since we were both waiting for people."

I couldn't believe it. I had always figured that Paula thought of me as kind of a social charity case, and that was why she was nice to me. But now it seemed that the Queen of the Sexies actually admired me. Maybe all the time I'd been wishing I could be sexy, like her, she would have liked to be smart, like me.

Was that the way it was, that the honors Creeps were too busy wishing they were sexy to get off on being smart? And the Sexies were too dumb to enjoy being sexy? Too bad for all of us.

Jack was saying something: "So I told Paula, 'I guess I'm pretty lucky to have met Diana Pushkin, girl wonder, on just my second day in town.' "

I started to feel hopeful. I was glad that Jimmy had given me that lesson under the willow tree. Suddenly, I remembered our conversation in the cafeteria. He had raised an eyebrow and said, "You felt like a WOMAN to me."

Paula Proomer wasn't Jack's type. Maybe *I* was.

The movie was a romantic musical set in the English countryside. It had pretty photography of farms and sunsets. Nina Castle did a great job of acting and singing, and naturally she looked beautiful. The movie was so good that after about fifteen minutes I forgot to worry about whether or not Jack would hold my hand. (He didn't.)

At the end, when the lights came on and the credits were rolling, Jack and I kept staring at the screen. As usual, it was hard for me to adjust to the fact that the movie was OVER. That I was no longer on the moors of England, but in downtown Bee-churst. People all around us were stretching, tripping over our knees to get by, discussing plans for eating ice cream, and humming the final song off-key.

The screen went blank, and Jack and I were just about the only ones still in their seats. I dreaded his breaking the mood by asking, "So, what did you think of the movie?" or "Wanna grab a pizza?"

"Let's go for a walk," he said.

"OK," I answered, still into the movie and not looking forward to having to make conversation. Also, I was scared that if I started talking, I would turn Jack off forever by launching into Nina Castle's English accent without intending to. I mean, the last time I saw Nina Castle in a movie, I was her for three days.

We made our way up the aisle, crunching popcorn under our feet, and out through the lobby.

"Listen, do you mind if we don't talk right away?" Jack asked suddenly. "I want to think about the movie for a while."

"I do too," I said, with only the slightest trace of an English accent.

"Later, when we 'come down' from the movie, we can talk about it. OK?" Jack said.

"Maybe in about ten years."

Jack laughed and put his arm around me. "I was thinking more along the lines of — say — ten minutes," he said.

"I'll try to be recovered by then too."

Our arms kind of drifted around each other, and we walked slowly down Main Street. No hurry at all.

I thought about the movie we had just seen. The music, the sad parts, the ending. . . . It's funny, but I didn't feel as if *I* were Nina Castle or the farmer's wife she had played, or even as if I were English. I didn't try to pretend I was Jacqueline Chase. Or Maxine Sanders. Or Julie Paris. Or Paula Proomer.

For the first time in a long time, I just felt like Diana Pushkin. And you know, it wasn't a bad way to feel.